Temperature's rising . . .

Reed turned again and looked at her. The moonlight shimmered in her eyes, and the light sea breeze lifted her beautiful blonde hair. He was fully aware of what he was feeling inside. . . .

"Reed?" someone shouted from up the beach.

Reed and Jess both turned. Paula was coming toward them.

Other Books by Todd Strasser:

The Diving Bell
Friends Till the End
The Accident
Home Alone™ (novelization)
Home Alone II™ (novelization)
The Mall from Outer Space
Beyond the Reef
The Complete Computer Popularity Program

**and the next book in the
LIFEGUARDS SERIES:**

Summer's End

Lifeguards

SUMMER'S PROMISE

TODD STRASSER

SCHOLASTIC INC.
New York Toronto London Auckland Sydney

ISBN 0-590-46966-5

12 11 10 9 8 7 6 5 4 3 2 1   3 4 5 6 7 8/9

Printed in the U.S.A.   01

First Scholastic printing, June 1993

For Joseph and Emily Levine

Thanks to Ron Masters and the Point Lookout lifeguards, my friends at the Larchmont Library, and Sheila Strasser for their help and assistance.

ONE

Jess Sloat's straight, sun-bleached blonde hair skipped in the morning breeze. Goose bumps ran up her long, tanned, bare legs, and the sleeves of her oversized navy-blue sweatshirt bunched up as she hugged herself and waited outside the lifeguard shack for the other guards to arrive.

Today was Jess's first day as a lifeguard and she was nervous. Of course, she'd completed CPR, first aid, and the two-week training course, and she'd always been a strong swimmer. But as Hank Diamond, the lifeguard captain, had said, there was a big difference between practice and the real thing.

Would she really be able to rescue a drowning person? Would she be accepted by the more experienced members of the Far Hampton lifeguard crew?

Jess looked back at the lifeguard shack, a small, two-room hut with brown weathered shingles

1

on its roof and large flakes of white paint peeling off the exterior walls. Despite the rickety exterior, Jess knew Hank kept a high-tech operation inside. At least, high-tech for lifeguards. There were two-way radios, electronic barometers, a computer, and other electronic equipment. All of which intimidated her.

She turned and gazed down the long strip of white beach and watched the blue ocean waves roll and curl in the clear bright sunlight. Their crashes were loud and rhythmic. In the distance, a lone, stocky figure jogged near the ocean's edge. Jess knew immediately that it was Andy, and she found comfort in the thought that he was a lifeguard, too.

Andy Moncure. Even though he was far away, and his face was hidden in the shadow of a hooded sweatshirt, she knew it was him. Always working harder than anyone else, always trying to better himself. In some ways Andy was the most serious and determined person she knew, but he tried to hide his seriousness behind a façade of jokes and humor.

Good old Andy. They'd been friends since forever. Through grade school and junior high and now high school. A couple of Far Hampton townies who hoped to do more with their lives than marry young, have lots of kids, and live off the tourist trade that came every summer. Maybe that was good enough for most of their classmates at Far Hampton High, but Jess and Andy had discovered long ago that they wanted something more. Although sometimes it was hard to say exactly what that "something more" was.

Despite her nervousness, Jess smiled as Andy turned away from the water's edge and jogged up the beach toward the lifeguard shack. Andy was a second-year guard, and well-liked by the other members of the crew. Jess hoped that once the crew found out that she and Andy were close friends, they would accept her, too.

A moment later Andy stopped a few feet from her and pulled the hood off his head. He'd cut his dark hair short. Short hair was the fad among the male lifeguards, and it looked good on some of them. But it made Andy's ears too big.

Andy breathed hard as he pressed his hands against the shack's wall and stretched his calves. Jess had always thought of him as having "square" looks. His square face, with its broad jaw and low forehead. His square shoulders that made him look like a football player, which he probably would have been, except that at 5'6" he was too small. It all combined to make him look reliable and dependable and built to last. She felt lucky to have him as a friend.

Andy turned to her and ran his hand over his hair. "What do you think?"

"It's different," Jess said. She'd never lie to Andy, but she didn't want to hurt his feelings, either.

Andy frowned. "That's all? Just different?"

"Well, it's a big change," Jess said carefully. "I'm going to have to get used to it."

Andy bent down his head. "Aw, Jess, I thought you were going to say you think it's great." He sounded very disappointed.

Jess put her hands on his muscular shoulders and looked straight at him. At 5'7" she was actually an inch taller than he was. "I do, Andy. And more important, I think *you're* great."

Andy raised his head and Jess looked into his brown eyes. His gaze was steady and almost questioning. Then he smiled.

"But we're just friends, right?" he said. He held up his hand for a high five and Jess slapped it. "Duh, we're just a couple a dumb townies, right?"

"Duh, dat's right," Jess replied with an exaggerated nod.

They shared a short laugh. Andy could always make her laugh.

"So, you psyched?" Andy said.

"Try nervous," Jess said.

"Nervous? Why?"

"Weren't you on *your* first day as a lifeguard?" Jess asked.

"Humm." Andy rubbed his chin and cocked an eye upward. "Let me try to remember. It was so long ago."

Jess punched him on the arm. "It was not. It was only last summer."

"And you think that wasn't a long time ago?"

Actually, Andy was right. It seemed like an eternity since last summer. Jess thought back to the previous year, when she'd been fifteen, and too young to be a lifeguard. Andy had turned sixteen at the beginning of the summer, so he was able to qualify. Jess had spent the whole summer waiting, watching, trying to do everything possible to prepare for the day when she'd be a lifeguard.

And now that day was here.

"I just can't believe it," Jess said. "Think I'll be okay?"

"Nope." Andy shook his head. "I hear you're way out of your league and doomed to failure."

"Andy . . ." Jess gave him an exasperated look. "Don't joke."

Andy grinned. "Don't worry, you'll do fine."

The next person to arrive was Ellie Sax, who was a fifth-year lifeguard going into her sophomore year at college. She rode up on a mountain bike. Ellie was wearing tight blue-and-black Spandex biking pants over her orange one-piece Far Hampton lifeguard bathing suit. Ellie had been a star on the Far Hampton swim and track teams for four straight years before going away to state college. She had broad shoulders and muscular arms and legs. Her long brown hair was always pulled back into a thick braid that fell past the middle of her back.

"Wow, she's been pumping iron at college," Andy whispered to Jess as they watched her get off her bike.

"You think?" Jess whispered back.

"Got to be," Andy whispered. "Don't you remember her last summer? I mean, she was in good shape, but nothing like this."

Ellie came over to greet them.

"Hi, Andy," she said, flashing her brilliant white smile and shaking his hand.

"Hey, not so hard!" Andy let his hand hang limp.

"Still joking," Ellie said, shaking her head. Then she turned to Jess. "Hi."

"Hi," Jess said.

"This is Jess Sloat," Andy introduced her.

"I think I remember seeing you around last summer," Ellie said.

"Last year she was a lifeguard groupie," Andy said. "This year she's part of the lifeguard group!"

Ellie rolled her eyes. "You haven't changed, Andy." She looked at Jess again. "But you look different."

"Late growth spurt, I guess," Jess said. "I added a few inches over the winter."

"And it wasn't just in height, either," Andy added.

"Andy!" Jess gave him a playful poke in the ribs.

"Hey, I can't help it if I'm a guy and notice things like that," Andy said. "Besides, that's not the only way you've changed. You let your hair grow longer and you started wearing a little makeup and those cute earrings. Basically you went from being pretty to being beautiful."

Jess felt her cheeks redden. She was surprised that Andy had been so observant.

"Well, it's good to have you on the crew, Jess,"

Ellie said. "If there's anything I can do, just yell."

"Thanks."

Ellie went back to her bike and Jess turned and eyed Andy suspiciously. "Beautiful, Andy?"

"In my humble opinion, totally." Andy nodded.

"How come you never said anything like that before?" Jess asked.

"You're my friend," Andy said. "I'm not supposed to notice. Or if I do, I'm not supposed to say anything."

"Says who?" Jess asked.

"I don't know." Andy shrugged. "So listen, maybe you'll get to sit with Ellie in one of the chairs. She's a really good guard. You could learn a lot."

Jess was surprised. "But I want to sit with you."

"You can't," Andy said. "Didn't Hank tell you that every chair has to have a senior guard? I'm hoping he'll make me one this year, but I haven't heard anything yet."

"Then who will I sit with?" Jess asked.

Andy shrugged. "That's up to Hank. You'll know pretty soon."

Several more guards Jess didn't know arrived, and then petite Lisa Jones came in a beat-up old Volkswagen. Like Jess, Lisa was a rookie and had gone through the training with her. She'd moved to town the previous year. Lisa was a shy girl with large dark eyes and straight black hair that was cut short and fell over her forehead in thick bangs. Jess didn't know her well, but she liked her. Lisa always wore a faded denim jacket with a red rose embroidered on the back. Jess had noticed that Lisa had a very shapely body but tried to hide it by wearing the jacket and baggy clothes. Likewise, she would have looked a lot prettier if she'd worn just a little makeup.

She quickly joined Jess and glanced shyly at Andy.

"Nervous?" she whispered to Jess.

"A little."

"God, I could hardly sleep last night," Lisa said. "I just kept thinking about rip currents and drop-offs and side carries and the right way to tie a bowline. I mean, how are we supposed to remember all that stuff?"

"Hank says it just becomes second nature after a while," Jess said.

"Maybe, if we're lucky, this will be the calmest summer in history," Lisa said wistfully. "No rogue waves, no sudden storms, no riptides."

"Hey, maybe the whole ocean will just dry up and we'll be the lifeguards of the desert," Andy suggested.

"Lisa Jones," Jess said, "this is Andy Moncure, my friend with the strange imagination."

"Howdy," Andy said.

"Oh, hi," Lisa said, staring wide-eyed at him. "You can't be a rookie, too."

"No, this is my tenth year," Andy replied. "I started when I was seven."

Lisa scowled.

"He likes to kid people," Jess explained, giving Andy a nudge. "This is his second year."

"Any advice?" Lisa asked.

"Sure, never listen to Hank or the senior guards," Andy said. "Whatever they tell you to do, do the exact opposite. And most importantly, don't try to save anyone unless they've gone down and come up at least three times. Now if you'll excuse me, ladies." He left them for a moment to drink some water from a spigot on the side of the lifeguard shack.

"What's his story?" Lisa whispered to Jess.

"Believe it or not, he's a really good guy," Jess said. "We've been friends since grade school. It's just that whenever he meets someone new, he feels like he has to be funny."

"You mean, like it's a defense mechanism or something?" Lisa asked.

"I guess," Jess said. "All I know is, once he gets to know you, he's a really solid friend."

Lisa looked back at Andy, who had bent down and was now splashing cold water from the spigot onto his face. "That would be nice," she said.

Hank Diamond arrived next, wearing a faded blue baseball jacket with Far Hampton Lifeguard stenciled on the back, and equally faded orange bathing trunks. He was the lanky, weathered lifeguard captain who'd been working on the beach at Far Hampton for more than fifteen years.

"Everyone here?" Hank asked, looking around at them from beneath his bushy, sun-bleached eyebrows.

"Everyone except the Petersens," Andy replied as he rejoined Jess and Lisa.

"So what else is new?" Hank said, turning away and using his key to open the heavy lock in the lifeguard shack door. "I just have to take care of a few things and then we'll get going." He went in and closed the door behind him.

"Who are the Petersens?" Lisa asked.

"Reed and Billy Petersen," Andy said without his usual humor. "A couple of rich kids from the city. They come out during the summer because their family has a mansion on the beach. Mr. Petersen is a big real-estate developer around here."

"If they're rich, why do they want to be life-guards?" Lisa asked.

"Who knows?" Andy said with a shrug. "Impress girls, I guess."

Lisa looked questioningly at Jess.

"I don't know them," Jess said. "I've just heard that they're both snobs and Billy's pretty wild."

No sooner were the words out of her mouth than a gun-metal-gray jeep came racing along the beach. It cut sharply toward them and then pulled up into the parking lot behind the life-guard shack and skidded to a stop. There were two guys inside. The one in the passenger seat was wearing reflective sunglasses, a black tank top, and loosely laced high-top basketball sneakers. His dark hair was cut short. Unlike the other lifeguards, he looked a bit pudgy and soft, as if he rarely exercised. As he got out of the jeep, he crushed his cigarette on the asphalt.

"That's Billy," Andy whispered.

Jess watched Reed Petersen climb out of the driver's seat. He was taller than Billy — probably a few inches more than six feet. She could see the muscle definition under his taut, tanned skin. He hadn't cut his chestnut-colored hair short, like the other lifeguards. Instead he kept it long and slightly wavy. He had handsome, chiseled looks, a high forehead, and a slim straight nose. He wore dark green Ray • Bans, a white sweatshirt with the sleeves rolled partway up, and deck shoes. Like his car, his clothes looked expensive.

Jess watched as Reed came toward them, followed by Billy. She actually knew more about Reed than she'd revealed to Lisa. A classmate of hers had dated him briefly the summer before. She'd said that Reed was moody, pensive, and mysterious. They'd gone out twice and then he'd never called again. Jess's friend heard something about Reed having a girlfriend who'd gone away for a few weeks and then came back. Her friend admitted she was very disappointed. Jess hadn't made any comments, but she wasn't surprised that Reed had left her high and dry. After all, Reed was a rich city kid. Like most kids she'd met from the city, he probably looked down on the year-round residents of Far Hampton. To the city kids, the residents of Far Hampton were townies and county bumpkins, to be played with and used, and then forgotten at the end of the summer. In a way, Jess thought her friend was lucky that Reed hadn't strung her along further, or hurt her more.

As the Petersen brothers joined the group, Hank Diamond came out of the lifeguard shack with a clipboard.

"I see we're all here now," Hank said, scanning the group. His gaze settled on Billy Petersen. "Billy, was that a cigarette I saw you smoking when you and your brother pulled in?"

"Uh, no, sir," Billy lied.

Hank smirked. "I'm glad. You know how I feel about lifeguards smoking around the beach. It definitely doesn't fit the image of competence and ability we want to present to the public. And talk about image, what's with the trunks?"

Everyone turned and looked at Billy's bathing trunks. Unlike the other male guards', Billy's weren't baggy. Instead, they were practically skin tight.

"I didn't think they looked good baggy, so I had Helene take them in," Billy explained.

"Who's Helene?" Hank asked.

"Our housekeeper."

Hank rolled up his eyes at the clear blue summer sky. "Well, tonight you give them back to Helene and tell her to put a little play back in them. You're wearing those trunks so that people will know you're a lifeguard, not a fashion plate."

Having finished with Billy, Hank turned to the rest of the group. "Okay, welcome to another summer at Far Hampton Beach. I'd especially like to welcome our two new rookies, Lisa Jones and Jess Sloat."

Jess felt self-conscious as the other lifeguards looked at her. She was especially aware of Billy Petersen, who'd tipped his reflecting sunglasses up and was staring at her with a slight leer.

"You've all been briefed on what to expect," Hank continued. "The only thing that remains are the chair assignments." Hank looked down at his clipboard and started reading off pairs of guards. Two experienced guards, Stu and Adam, were assigned to the Malibu chair way down the beach. Two others, a girl named Chris and a guy named Al, were assigned to the Dunes chair way down in the opposite direction near the Sandy Dunes motel. That left the three chairs more or less in front of the lifeguard shack.

"Ellie Sax and Lisa Jones are in the West Wing chair," Hank said. "Billy Petersen and Andy Moncure have the East Wing."

Jess noticed that Billy was still staring at her.

"Uh, excuse me, Hank," Andy waved his hand. "If it's me and Billy, there's no senior guard in that chair."

"I'm promoting Billy to senior guard," Hank said. "This is his third year and he deserves a chance."

Billy stopped staring at Jess and smiled proudly at the promotion. Jess noticed that no one congratulated him. Beside her, Andy hung his head in disappointment. He must have been hoping Hank would name him, not Billy, as senior guard to that chair.

"So why don't you take a moment to shake hands with your new partners," Hank said, putting down the clipboard.

Suddenly, Jess was worried. Lisa had already turned to talk to Ellie, so Jess grabbed Andy's arm before he went to talk to Billy.

"What is it?" Andy asked.

"Hank didn't assign me to a chair," Jess whispered.

"See?" Andy said. "I told you he didn't think you were fit to lifeguard."

"You're kidding, right?" Jess whispered nervously. "I mean, that can't really be true."

"Of course not," Andy reassured her. "Don't be a nut case. You've been assigned."

"How? He didn't say anything."

"It's a simple process of elimination," Andy said. "The only chair left is the Main chair. And the only guard left is . . ."

Before Andy could finish, Jess felt someone tap her on the shoulder. She turned around and looked up into Reed Petersen's dark eyes and handsome tanned face.

"Hi," he said, extending his hand. "I'm Reed Petersen."

TWO

"Hi." Jess shook his hand and tried not to show the nervousness that washed over her. Why did Reed Petersen make her feel that way? He was just another rich, good-looking guy from the city. Every summer brought loads of them, living in their parents' fancy summer homes, cruising around town in their fast cars, and generally strutting around as if they thought they were the greatest things on earth. She'd met plenty of them before. This was nothing new.

"You must have done well in training," Reed said, focusing his intense eyes on her.

"Why?"

"Because Hank usually doesn't put rookies in the Main chair," Reed said. "He usually puts them out in the wings where it's less crowded."

"I guess I'm just lucky," Jess replied with a shrug. The truth was she would have preferred to sit with anyone rather than Reed or his brother, Billy.

"We'll see," Reed said.

Jess wanted to ask him what he meant by that, but before she could, Hank gathered everyone together. "Okay, first order of business this morning will be a one-mile run. When you get back, the daily chart will be posted on the bulletin board, pointing out the danger spots. I want everyone to study it and then get in their chairs."

As Reed Petersen started off along the wet sand at the ocean's edge, he found himself falling into step with Ellie Sax. She and Reed had shared a wing chair their first year together and they'd been good friends ever since.

They took a few moments to catch up with each other. Ellie talked about how her college weight-training program had helped shave a few tenths off her swimming times. Then she asked Reed about St. Peter's, the private school he and Billy went to.

"Billy's not there anymore," Reed said.

"What happened?"

"He, uh, decided to go somewhere else," Reed said.

Ellie glanced over and gave him a knowing look. "You're funny, Reed."

"Why's that?"

"You're so protective of everyone. Billy wouldn't just leave St. Peter's. But you'll never tell the real reason."

She was right. Billy had been thrown out of school for drinking and breaking curfew. But Reed wouldn't tell anyone that.

"Sometimes I think you're a better brother than Billy deserves," Ellie said.

A year before Reed would have argued in defense of his brother. But this past year Billy had changed, going from a goofy clown to a mean, angry, and unpredictable kid with a penchant for getting into trouble.

"What do you think of Hank making him a senior guard?" Ellie asked.

"Everyone deserves a chance," Reed replied. But he understood Ellie's concern. Being a senior guard meant being responsible for the lives of a lot of patrons, which was what the lifeguards called the people who used the beach. While the guards generally worked in pairs off each chair, in a large emergency they all had to chip in. A weak link could prove fatal.

"You know anything about the two rookies?" Reed asked.

"I think the one named Lisa is new in town," Ellie replied as they ran. "I don't know much about her. But I'm pretty sure the other one, Jess Sloat, is a strong swimmer. You should be okay with her. She probably has a pretty good idea of what to do. Don't you remember she was always hanging around Andy's chair last summer?"

Reed looked back over his shoulder. Jess was about twenty yards behind them, running with Andy Moncure. Now that he thought about it, he did remember seeing her the year before, but he didn't remember her looking quite so pretty, or being quite so tall and curvy. Not that it mattered. She'd stuck to Andy like glue the previous year and it was obvious that they were still together.

And besides, he was supposed to be with Paula.

Twenty yards behind Reed and Ellie, Jess ran with Andy. The sun was rising higher in the sky and the air was getting warmer. Jess could feel the sun's strong rays on the backs of her legs, and she was starting to get hot under her sweatshirt.

"Give me a yell if I'm going to step on a horse-shoe crab or something," Jess said. Then, without breaking stride, she pulled her sweatshirt up over her head and tied it around her waist. The ocean breeze felt cool against the bare skin of her arms and shoulders.

Andy jogged silently beside her. He had hardly said a word since learning that Billy was going to be his senior guard. Jess knew that he could spend the whole day sulking if she didn't get him out of it.

"You're really that upset that Hank made Billy senior guard?"

"In a word? Yes," Andy said.

"Maybe he was the next in line," Jess replied.

"Get crucial, Jess," Andy said. "The guy's always getting into trouble. Half the time he's so busy scoping girls that he forgets to watch the patroons."

Andy always said "patroons" instead of patrons.

"Besides," Andy continued. "Hank knows how hard I worked last summer. He should have made me a senior guard. Then you and I could share a chair and — " He didn't finish the sentence.

"And what?" Jess asked.

"Nothing."

"Tell me, Andy."

"And you wouldn't have to share a chair with Reed Petersen."

For the next few moments they jogged along the water's edge in silence. Jess knew what Andy was referring to. She wasn't thrilled about sharing a chair with Reed Petersen, either. In general she tried to steer clear of the city kids and stick with her own kind. But maybe something good would come of it.

"Won't I learn a lot?" Jess asked. "I mean, Reed must have almost as much experience as Ellie."

"Sure, you'll learn a lot," Andy replied. "Probably about fast cars and wild parties and running up huge credit card bills."

"I didn't know you had something against fast cars and wild parties."

Andy had to smile as he huffed and puffed beside her. "Sure. If it's my car and a party I'm invited to, I think it's great."

"I know Reed and Billy are rich and from the city," Jess said. "But is there something else about them you don't like?"

"I guess they're just majorly into everything I despise," Andy said. "They're not just rich. They're the richest, the snobbiest, and the dirtiest fighters. People around here say Petersen-Lewis is the toughest company they've ever done business with. They always have to squeeze blood from a stone."

"What's Petersen–Lewis?" Jess asked.

"Their land development company," Andy said. "Mr. Petersen and a guy named Bernard Lewis are partners in it. You've seen Paula Lewis, right?"

"I'm not sure," Jess said. "What does she look like?"

"You're serious?" Andy looked surprised. "You can't miss her. She's about the same size as your friend, Lisa, and she's got the same kind of dark hair, but that's where the similarity ends. All you have to do is look for the smallest bikini and the most gold jewelry and you'll find her. The biggest tragedy of Paula's life is when the paint chips off one of her fingernails."

"Sounds like my kind of girl," Jess said sarcastically.

"Wait, I'm not finished," Andy said. "Now pretend you're seventeen and you're so rich you can have any kind of car you want. What would you get?"

"Well . . ." Jess had to think about it for a moment. "I guess it wouldn't matter as long as it ran."

"No, no!" Andy cried. "Pretend you're to-tally *rich*. You could have *any car you wanted*."

"But I really wouldn't care," Jess said. Jess

had just gotten her junior license, but neither she nor her parents could afford to get her a car.

"God, you're no fun." Andy wiped the sweat off his brow and shook his head. They'd reached the half-mile mark, time to turn around and head back to the lifeguard shack. "I mean, you could have a Porsche or a Ferrari or a lunar space module if you wanted."

"I think you'd better get to the point, Andy."

"Okay, Paula Lewis is rich enough to have any car she wants and you know what she drives?" Andy asked. "A *Cadillac!*"

"I think I'm getting the picture," Jess said.

"You're going to get it a lot better," Andy said. "Paula is Reed's girlfriend. And she never lets him out of her sight."

By the time Jess and Andy returned to the lifeguard shack, Jess had decided to ask Hank to change her chair assignment. She knew it was a lot to ask, especially for a rookie, but she had good reasons. Of course, she couldn't tell Hank the *main* reason, which was that she didn't want to sit with Reed Petersen or be around his girlfriend, Paula. Instead she would tell Hank that she didn't think it was a good idea for a rookie to sit in the busiest chair on the beach.

The door of the lifeguard shack was closed, and as Jess stepped up onto the porch, she could hear Hank's voice.

"Now I'm going to be straight with you, Billy," Hank was saying in a stern voice. "I'm sticking my neck out by making you a senior guard. It's a lot of responsibility and I don't want you to let me down. Understand?"

"Yeah."

"Okay, now next time I assign a one-mile run, you do it," Hank said. "I don't want to come out again and find you hiding behind the dunes, trying to get out of it."

"Okay, Hank."

"Good, now get out and do that run."

The door to the shack opened and Billy came out. When he saw Jess, he stopped. For a moment they just stared at each other. Then Billy smiled.

"Waiting for someone?"

"I was just waiting to speak to Hank," Jess replied. She hated the way he looked at her. As if he were undressing her with his eyes. And what was really infuriating was that he didn't try to sneak it. He was so bold he just stood there and stared.

"Maybe we could get together sometime," Billy said.

"Maybe," Jess said uncomfortably. The answer was actually a resounding *NO!* but he seemed like the kind of boy who didn't take no for an answer.

Billy left the porch and Jess knocked on the door.

"Come in!" Hank shouted.

Jess pushed the door open. Inside, Hank was sitting at his desk doing some paperwork. On the table beside him were half a dozen different radios and telephones — direct lines to the police, paramedics, and local hospitals. On the walls were oceanographic charts and bulletins about everything from stinging jellyfish to new techniques for removing fishhooks from people's feet. Past Hank's desk was a broad glass window so that he could look out and see the beach.

Hank looked up at her. "Hey, Jess, what's up?"

"I was wondering if I could talk to you about something," Jess said, closing the door behind her.

"Okay, have a seat." Hank pointed to a beat-up wooden chair pushed in against a desk with a computer on it.

"So what's on your mind?" Hank asked.

Jess felt her heart begin to race. She'd never been good at asking for things for herself. "Well,

I was wondering if I could sit in a different chair."

Hank's eyebrows went up. "Something wrong with the Main chair?"

"Not really," Jess said. "I just think it's a lot of responsibility for someone brand new."

"I understand how you feel, Jess," Hank replied. "But I wouldn't have assigned you there if I didn't think you could handle it."

"But you yourself said there was a big difference between practicing lifesaving and real lifesaving," Jess said.

"Absolutely," Hank said. "But you'll be under Reed's supervision and he's about as good a lifeguard as you're going to find. Now let me assure you, Jess, I put a lot of thought into these assignments. If I didn't think you were right for the Main chair, I wouldn't have put you there."

Jess's insides were aswirl. Here she was, brand new at the job, and the last thing she wanted to do was make trouble. There were two voices in her head. One of them was telling her to forget about asking for another chair assignment. The other kept warning her that sitting with Reed Petersen would only lead to trouble.

"Don't lifeguards ever have a say about what chair they're assigned to?" Jess asked.

"In certain situations," Hank replied. "Like if

there was something that would prevent two guards from working well together. Like a personality conflict."

Jess decided to take a chance. "It's partly that," she said.

Hank looked surprised, but before he could say anything, Jess heard a noise from the back room. She looked around and noticed that the door was partly open. Reed Petersen was standing there, staring at her.

THREE

<u>H</u>e must have heard every word, Jess thought, feeling a blush race across her cheeks. Reed's expression was a handsome mask. She couldn't tell what he was thinking. In his hands he held a thick red tube with a rope attached. It was a torpedo buoy, used in certain kinds of rescues.

"You fix that torp?" Hank asked.

Reed nodded and leaned the buoy in the doorway. He glanced again at Jess and then back to Hank. "Maybe she's right, Hank."

"You serious, Reed?" Hank looked surprised.

"Well, I don't know about the personality conflict," Reed said, glancing back at Jess. "But if she doesn't feel she's up to the job, why take a chance?"

Jess felt a sudden burst of anger. Who was *he* to decide whether or not she could do the job? "I never said I wasn't up to it," she said.

Reed turned slowly and studied her. Unlike

Andy, he never seemed to react to anything quickly. He always seemed to take his time and consider the situation fully.

"That's not what I just heard you say?" Reed asked.

"No." Jess shook her head angrily and got up. "You must have been mistaken. Maybe next time you eavesdrop you should leave the door open more so you can hear things more clearly."

Jess turned and went out. The last thing in the world she was going to admit, especially to some stuck-up city boy, was that she was a little bit scared of the job.

Reed watched her march out and close the door behind her.

"I didn't realize you two knew each other," Hank said.

"That's what's weird, Hank," Reed said. "We don't."

"But she said something about a personality conflict," Hank said. "Maybe you *should* know her, and that's why she's mad." He burst into song. "Some enchanted evening . . ."

Reed smirked, then shook his head. "It's morning, Hank. And believe me, it's nothing like that."

"I believe you, Reed. Besides, you've got too much style," Hank teased.

"I've never talked to her in my life," Reed said. "Except to say hello this morning. Maybe she doesn't like the way I shake hands." Reed glanced out the window and then back at Hank. "You sure she can handle the Main chair?"

The captain nodded. "It's just first-week nerves, Reed. Give her some time. I'm pretty sure she's solid."

Reed didn't argue. He'd worked under Hank for three years and he knew the lifeguard captain gave people the chance to prove themselves. Hank had done it for Reed when he was a rookie, too. It was something Reed had always appreciated. Except for today.

Through the window, Reed could see the first patrons starting to spread their blankets on the sand. "Guess it's time to get in the chair," he said.

"Just a minute," Hank said. "I've got something here I want to show you."

Out on the beach, Jess stepped over the ropes that separated the Main chair from the rest of the beach where the patrons could sit. The Main chair was on a wooden stand six feet high and was built on top of a four-foot mound of sand, so the guard was actually ten feet above the beach. The chair was painted white and the seat was slightly narrower than a park bench. Jess climbed up the white ladder and sat down in the corner of the chair.

She liked being high up in the chair. The view of the beach and ocean was wonderful. She could feel the moist onshore breeze on her face, and way out on the sparkling blue water she could see the dark shape of an oil tanker inching along the horizon. Looking up and down the beach, she could see for miles in either direction. But her concern that day would be a much smaller area — the beach for roughly fifty yards in either direction and the waters it faced.

Jess looked to her right. More patrons were arriving and a few multicolored umbrellas were going up. One or two bathers were standing at the water's edge, sticking a toe in, but no one had started swimming yet. In the distance, she could see the West Wing chair. The wing chairs were about the same size as the Main chair, but they stood on lower mounds of sand. As Jess looked, she could see Lisa sitting next to Ellie.

She turned and looked to her left. About twenty yards away, an area of beach was marked with red flags, warning patrons to stay away. There was a rip current there, a depression where waves converged and the undertow was unusually strong. An unsuspecting swimmer could get caught in it and be quickly swept twenty or thirty yards offshore. Only a strong swimmer would be able to swim back unaided.

Beyond the red flags, Jess could see Billy Petersen and Andy in the East Wing chair. Because of the red flags, the East Wing chair got the fewest number of patrons. Jess suspected that that was why Hank had stationed Billy and Andy there. Some days hardly anyone spread a blanket or swam off that part of the beach. Jess sighed. She wished she were sitting with Andy.

Reed left the lifeguard shack and jogged toward the Main chair. Hank had just shown him the literature on the new Doppler radar. As Hank explained it, the Doppler radar would help detect developing thunderstorms and would give the lifeguards extra time to clear the beach. Sudden thunderstorms were a real headache for lifeguards. The unexpected winds blew umbrellas and towels all over the place, but much worse, there was a report of someone on a beach being hit by lightning and killed every few years.

Reed thought the new radar would be a great help for the lifeguard crew, but right now he had a more immediate concern, a rookie lifeguard

with a questionable attitude. It was important
that he and Jess Sloat reach some kind of understanding. Other people's lives were going to
depend upon it.

Jess didn't notice Reed until he was already
partway up the ladder. Several swimmers had
started venturing into the water and she was
keeping an eye on them, especially one who
showed signs of being a potential problem. Reed
reached the top of the ladder and slid onto the
chair. Jess had hoped that he'd hug the opposite
corner of the chair, but instead he sat down about
halfway between the corner and where she was
sitting.

"How's it going?" he asked loudly over the
crashing of the waves. He didn't look at her as
he spoke. Instead his eyes were already scanning
the beach and the water. In lifeguarding you had
to talk to your partner without looking at him.
Look away from the water for one moment and
you might miss someone in trouble.

"Okay," Jess answered uncomfortably, staring at the edge of the beach. She still couldn't
believe he'd overheard her talking to Hank. She
told herself she had to stop thinking about that
and concentrate on the "potential" she'd just
spotted. A potential was anyone on the beach

who might pose a problem for the lifeguards. The potential she was concerned about was a rail-thin boy wearing cutoff jeans, standing knee deep in the foamy white surf, a dozen feet from five-foot waves that were curling and crashing on the sand.

"Any potentials?" Reed asked.

"One over there." Jess nodded toward the boy. "In the cutoff jeans."

"What's the problem?" Reed asked.

The problem had to be obvious, and Jess realized Reed was testing her. She began to feel a certain amount of resentment.

"Well, the cutoffs could mean he doesn't own a bathing suit, which would imply that he might not be a good swimmer."

"Or he just thinks cutoffs are cool," Reed countered.

"He's also really pale," Jess said. "Which could mean he hasn't spent much time outdoors swimming."

"True, but it's the beginning of the season," Reed said. "This might just be his first time out."

Jess couldn't help feeling a little annoyed. "He's also really thin, so I doubt he could swim against a strong current."

"You could be right about that," Reed said.

Jess smiled to herself. "Did I pass the test?"

"I'd say you did pretty well," Reed replied with a slight smile. On the beach, the boy apparently thought better of venturing out into the rough waves and headed back toward his blanket. It was the sort of thing that happened a hundred times a day, but you always had to be alert.

"How long are you going to keep testing me?" Jess asked Reed as she scanned the beach and water for any more potentials.

"Until I'm sure you know your stuff," Reed replied.

"I did just complete the training course," Jess reminded him.

"This is different," Reed said. "Here people's lives are at stake."

Jess knew that. She was tempted to ask why he cared so much about other people's lives, since it didn't have anything to do with meeting girls and looking cool.

"Excuse me," someone said.

Jess looked down to her left and saw a woman with a young boy, who was standing on one foot.

"My son stepped on a piece of glass and cut his foot," the woman said. "Do you have a Band-Aid?"

"Sure." Jess climbed down from the chair. The little boy was about five years old. He had brownish hair and the scrawny look of someone who'd recently lost his baby fat. As he held his mother's hand and watched Jess, she could see that he was on the verge of tears, but trying to fight it.

Jess opened the equipment box under the chair and took out the first-aid kit.

"Is it going to hurt?" the boy asked with a trembling voice.

"It shouldn't," Jess said as she took out the disinfectant. "And it's going to make the cut all better."

"I think it's going to hurt," the boy whimpered and clung to his mother's leg.

"Don't be a baby, Danny," the mother said harshly, trying to pry his hands off her leg.

"But I'm scared," Danny cried.

The mother shook her head impatiently. "When are you going to grow up?"

Jess thought she was being unfair. But it wasn't her business to interfere. Jess kneeled down so that she was at Danny's eye level.

"Danny?" she said softly.

Danny hid behind his mother's leg and wouldn't look at her.

"Danny, look." Jess opened the top of the disinfectant bottle and dabbed some on the back of her hand. "See? It's not so bad."

Danny peeked out from behind his mother's leg.

"Why don't you just touch it?" Jess asked.

Danny shook his head.

"Look." Jess touched the disinfectant with the tip of her finger. "See? And it's going to make your cut all better."

Gradually, with a lot more gentle coaxing, Jess got Danny to let her put the disinfectant on the cut and bandage it.

"Is it over?" Danny asked.

"Yes, Danny, and you were very brave." Danny grinned proudly and Jess rubbed his head affectionately. Danny's mother led her son away without even saying thanks. Jess climbed back up onto the lifeguard stand.

"Nice job," Reed said as he scanned the water and beach. It was growing warmer and more patrons were starting to go into the surf.

"If I didn't know better, I would have thought it was another test," Jess said. She quickly glanced over and saw Reed smile.

"That's right. I called Central Casting for one injured boy and mom," he said.

"If it's not a test, what do you call it?" Jess asked.

"Doing what you're paid to do," Reed said.

Even though lifeguarding was a job, Jess never

thought of it as something she did for money. It was just something she'd always wanted to do. Something she probably would have done for free had she not needed to save money for college. Again, she wondered why someone like Reed Petersen would be a lifeguard. It wasn't for the money, and she wasn't sure she believed Andy's theory that Reed did it to impress girls. Anyone as rich and handsome as Reed didn't need to be a lifeguard to do that.

"Now that you've shown what you can do with little kids, let's see what you can do with the big ones," Reed said, pointing toward the restricted area where the red flags were. A boogie boarder was riding the waves.

"Isn't it your turn?" Jess asked. Despite the fact that he was her senior guard, she'd never been one to take orders easily.

"It would be, except I've got my eye on another potential." Reed gestured to a head bobbing in the water beyond the breaking surf.

"I'll watch him," Jess said.

"I want you to take care of the boogie boarder," Reed replied. "You never know. Maybe it's another test."

Always obey your senior guard's orders. That was the rule. Jess climbed down from the stand and headed for the restricted area.

From a distance, Jess guessed that the kid on the boogie board was about twelve years old. He was wearing long, baggy, green bathing trunks and skimming in and under the big waves, sometimes getting caught and rolling in the surf and then kicking back out to catch the next wave.

The sand felt warm as Jess walked across it. As she neared the red flags, she put her whistle in her mouth and blew a long shrill warning. The boy quickly looked up.

Jess waved at him to come in, but he seemed to ignore her. Jess blew her whistle again. Now the boy caught a wave and started to ride it in, skillfully executing a 360-degree spin on the top of the wave and then shooting out through the tube.

"Nice move, but you're in a restricted area," Jess informed him as he trudged up the beach toward her, dragging his boogie board behind him. Out of the water, his long blond hair hung in strings over his eyes.

"But this is where the groovinest waves are," the boy said. His hair was cut very short on the sides, but was much longer on top. He wore a gold hoop earring, and many colorful rope bracelets braided around his wrists and ankles.

"I'm sorry, but it's off-limits," Jess said.

The boy just stared at her and grinned a big toothy grin. "Wow, you're a real babe."

His words caught Jess off guard. She couldn't help smiling. "And you're only twelve."

"Hey, how'd you know?" the boy asked.

"Just a guess."

"Well, that doesn't mean I don't notice stuff," the boy said. He extended a wet, sandy hand. "I'm Gary Pilot. What's your name?"

"Jess Sloat."

The boy looked surprised. "Like in Chief Sloat, the police chief?"

Jess nodded. "He's my father."

"Way cool. The next time I see him, I'll have to tell him he's got one beautiful babe daughter."

"Do you see a lot of my father?" Jess asked as she fought to keep a smile off her lips.

Gary shrugged and gave her a sly grin. "Uh, let's just say we run into each other now and then."

Jess could just imagine. "Okay, Gary, it's nice to meet you. You can boogie board on any other part of the beach. Just watch out for swimmers." Jess turned and started back toward the lifeguard stand.

"But what about the waves?" Gary asked behind her.

Jess stopped and turned. "There are waves all up and down the beach."

"But those waves are the pits, and these are totally excellent," Gary said, pointing back at the waves inside the red flags.

It was true that the water around a rip current was often rougher than any place else. But that wasn't the point.

"I'm sorry, Gary," Jess said. "But you can't swim here."

"Why not? I'm careful," Gary said.

Suddenly Jess heard a short burst from a whistle. She looked back at the stand. Reed was waving to her and saying something. Jess couldn't hear him over the crashing of the waves, but she'd always been pretty good at reading lips. Right now, Reed's lips appeared to be saying, "Let's get a move on."

Jess turned back to Gary. "It has nothing to do with being careful. This area is off-limits."

"Who decides that?"

Jess explained that Hank surveyed the beach each morning and decided where the dangerous spots were. But Gary kept asking questions, challenging her. He wasn't nasty or belligerent. In fact, he was polite and even funny at times. But he wouldn't take no for an answer.

Reed whistled from the lifeguard stand again. Jess knew he was probably wondering why she was taking so long.

"Look, Gary," she said finally. "You seem like a nice kid and I'd love to stand here and chat with you, but I can't. I have other things to do and you just have to find another place to surf."

"But I keep trying to tell you, there is no other place," Gary argued.

Suddenly Jess felt someone behind her and turned. It was Reed.

"Hey, Gary, how's it going?" Reed said, giving the boogie boarder a high five.

"Cool, Reed. How about you?"

"Can't complain," Reed said. "Now what's the problem?"

"Well, I was just trying to explain to this bodacious babe lifeguard that this whole beach has bogus waves except for right here," Gary explained.

"But she told you this is off-limits, didn't she?" Reed asked.

"Well, sure, but she doesn't know who I am," Gary said.

"Gary's probably the best boogie boarder on the whole south shore," Reed told Jess. "I've come out here and found him riding waves in hurricanes."

"See?" Gary said proudly. "And compared to a hurricane, these waves are like in diapers."

"But rules are rules, Gary," Reed said. "This is a restricted area and there's no swimming or surfing allowed. If I see you go back in here I'll have to get the shore police to remove you."

"But, Reed, man — " Gary started to protest.

"*No* arguments." Reed turned and walked back to the lifeguard stand. Jess followed him.

Back in the chair, Reed began to scan the beach and water again. Jess glanced back at Gary Pilot. He was still standing where they'd left him and for a second Jess wondered if he was going to challenge Reed's authority and start boogie boarding in the restricted area again. But after a few moments, Gary shrugged and dragged his board away toward another part of the beach. Why had he listened to Reed and not to her?

"You're too nice," Reed said, as if he were reading her mind.

"Hank says we should keep a cordial relationship with the patrons," Jess responded.

"Sure, but you have to learn to be firm," Reed said.

"I thought I was firm," Jess said. "He just wouldn't listen."

"Maybe because he saw that he could flatter you with that 'bodacious babe' stuff," Reed said.

"You can't be a good lifeguard if you're going to stand around listening to people tell you how pretty you are."

Reed's words stung even though Jess knew he was right. It was the first time in her life anyone had ever held her looks against her. Who did Reed Petersen think he was?

FOUR

Jess and Reed hardly said a thing to each other for the rest of the day. Jess didn't mind. It was better to sit in silence than hear how vain she was. Not that there was a lot for her to do. As Hank had told her a hundred times, the best lifeguards are the ones who rarely make rescues. They don't have to, because they practice preventive lifeguarding, which means warning people of dangerous situations before they get into trouble.

After work, Lisa offered to give Jess and Andy a ride home and they were glad to accept. Both of them lived far from the public beach and had to take the town bus each morning. They got into Lisa's VW, Jess sitting in the passenger seat and Andy in back. Lisa pulled up the sleeves of her denim jacket and put the car in gear.

"How about some tunes?" Andy asked, reaching between Lisa and Jess and flicking on the radio. A funky rap song came on.

"Is that what you listen to?" Andy asked with obvious distaste.

"What's wrong with it?" Lisa asked as she pulled out of the parking lot.

"It's not heavy metal," Jess said. "That's the only thing Andy listens to."

"Okay, forget it," Andy said, turning down the radio volume. "So who wants to go first?"

"Go where?" Lisa asked.

"He means talk about what happened today," Jess explained.

"Jess is just being nice," Andy said. "What I really mean is dish the dirt on what a jerk your senior guard is."

"But Ellie's nice," Lisa said.

In the back, Andy groaned. "Well, then make something up. No one wants to hear about how nice people are."

In the front Lisa gave Jess a puzzled glance.

"He's just pulling your leg," Jess said. "If Ellie was nice, then she was nice."

The beach road was lined with restaurants, resorts, and motels. "That looks like a cool place," Lisa said, pointing at the motel directly beside the public beach. The motel was painted pink with aqua trim.

"That's the Sandy Dunes," Andy said. "Every year they have a total blowout beach party with a live band and everything."

"It's one of the major highlights of the summer," Jess said.

"And what about that place?" Lisa asked, now pointing at a large white mansion with a fountain in front and a gate with a guard. On the grounds they could see people in white outfits playing tennis on clay courts.

"That's the Shore Club," Andy said. "Playground of the rich and famous." He tapped Jess on the shoulder. "Your buddy Reed Petersen and his family belong there."

"How do you know that?" Lisa asked.

"A friend of mine named Donny works there every summer," Andy said. "He's like a waiter and valet parker."

Ahead on the right was a low red restaurant with a green-and-white awning and a sign that said Crab Shack.

"Hey, I'm seriously thirsty," Andy said. "Anyone want to stop?"

Lisa and Jess glanced at each other.

"Sounds good," Jess said.

Lisa pulled into the Crab Shack's dirt parking lot. The VW bounced in and out of a few large potholes. They got out and sat down at a picnic table set out under the awning and ordered a pitcher of soda.

"So thanks to Lisa, we know Ellie was nice," Andy said, gazing at Jess. "What's up with Reed?"

"I get the feeling you really want to tell us about Billy," Jess said. "Why don't you go first?"

"Got a few days?" Andy asked.

"Maybe you should just give us the highlights," Jess said.

Andy took a long gulp of soda and put down his glass. "Okay, where do I start? How about the first thing this morning? You know how Hank promoted him to senior guard and then sent us out for that one-mile run?"

"I know he got into trouble," Jess said. "Because when I went into the shack Hank was bawling him out."

"You got it," Andy said. "He's been a senior guard for about a minute and the first thing he does is duck into the dunes so he doesn't have to do the whole run. So you think he learned his lesson? No way. We get out to the chair and he takes this little radio out of his shirt. So of course I feel it's my duty as a lifeguard to remind him that you're not allowed to listen to music while you're in the chair and he tells me to mind my own business."

"Should you tell Hank?" Lisa asked.

"Forget it," Andy said. "If I do, Billy will know who squealed. I mean, forget the fact that he's my senior guard and could make my life miserable. We're talking about a guy who'd be waiting for you in a dark alley with a baseball bat."

"Get serious," Jess said.

"I *am* serious," Andy said. "He does stuff like that."

"Why?" Lisa asked.

"Because he's rich Billy Petersen," Andy said. "His father practically owns Far Hampton. As far as he's concerned, the rules were made for someone else."

Andy took another sip of soda and looked up at Jess. "So tell us about brother Reed."

Jess shrugged. "There's nothing to tell."

"Nothing?" Andy looked surprised.

"It seems like he takes lifeguarding very seriously," Jess said.

"Don't believe it, Jess," Andy said. "It's just an act. That guy's so competitive. He has to be the best at everything. It's like he has to be king and make sure everyone worships him. He's even got Hank snowed."

"How?" Lisa asked.

Andy thought for a moment. "Okay, here's

an example. You know how much valuable electronic equipment there is in the lifeguard shack?"

The girls nodded.

"Well," Andy said, "there's only one spare
key. And guess who has it?"

"Reed?" Jess guessed.

"Right," Andy said.

"So what does that prove?" Lisa asked.

Andy looked surprised. "Isn't it obvious? It's
Reed's way of letting everyone know Hank
thinks he's the top lifeguard. I mean, there was
no way he was going to let anyone else get that
key."

Jess heard what her friend was saying, but she
wasn't certain she believed him. She'd sat with
Reed the whole day. Apart from that crack about
her looks, the only thing she'd seen him do was
his job.

The conversation drifted to other subjects and
then it was time to head home.

The town of Far Hampton was about two
miles from the beach. For years it had been a
one-street town with a bank, post office, grocery
store, hardware store, and a few other shops.
Then Charles Petersen had discovered it and
started buying up the farmland around the town
and building expensive summer homes only
people from the city could afford. And now the

once sleepy little town of Far Hampton featured
three streets of expensive clothing boutiques, an-
tique stores, premium ice-cream shops, and an
aerobics studio.

"There, that's where I live," Andy said as they
drove down Main Street.

"In the hardware store?" Lisa asked, puzzled.

"No, in the apartment over it," Andy said.
Lisa pulled over to the curb and Andy got out.
"See you guys tomorrow. And let's try to come
up with some better gossip, okay?"

They waved and headed for Jess's house.

"How come he lives over the hardware store?"
Lisa asked.

"His mom and dad split up when he was
about five," Jess said. "His mom's a waitress at
Alfredo's."

"That fancy Italian restaurant that always has
limousines in front of it?" Lisa said.

"You got it."

Jess and her family lived in a small, neatly kept
ranch house on the other side of town.

"It's the green house," Jess said, pointing
down the street.

"Uh-oh, I think you've got a problem," Lisa
said.

"Why?" Jess asked.

"There's a police car in your driveway."

"That's my father," Jess said. "He's the chief of police."

"Oh." Lisa stopped on the street. "Guess I'd better watch my driving around here."

Jess reached for the door handle and then stopped and turned back to Lisa. "So you never really told us how *your* first day went."

"Okay, I guess," Lisa said. "I mean, all I did was tell some guys they couldn't play football in the water and help one lost little girl find her mother."

It seemed to Jess that she sounded disappointed. "It's not what you expected, huh?"

"Oh, I don't know," Lisa said with a shrug. "I'm not sure what I expected." Then she smiled a little. "I just thought it would be better than spending the summer working at McDonald's, you know?"

Jess laughed. "Yes, I know." She started to reach for the car door, but Lisa stopped her.

"Can I ask you a question?"

"Okay."

"How come Andy's so down on Reed and Billy Petersen? I mean, it really sounds like he hates them."

"I don't think he really hates them," Jess said. "But there've been a couple of times when kids from the city were snobby to Andy. Sometimes

I think he's kind of defensive because they all seem to have so much money while he and his mom have to live in that apartment. Some of the things his mom overhears at Alfredo's are pretty outrageous."

"Like what?" Lisa asked.

"Oh, just what they spend on their beach houses and their private planes. Things like that," Jess said.

"It's funny about Andy," Lisa said. "Because he seems like a really nice guy."

"Andy? He's the best."

Lisa fingered the collar of her denim jacket. "You think maybe he's a little jealous?"

"Of what?" Jess asked.

"Of you sitting with Reed Petersen?"

Jess looked across at Lisa in amazement. "Why would Andy be jealous of me and Reed?"

"Well, Reed is gorgeous and rich," Lisa said.

Jess smiled. "So are about a hundred other guys you'll meet this summer. No, I can't imagine Andy being jealous. He knows me too well."

"You did say you were old friends."

"Since grade school," Jess said. "Maybe even since kindergarten, but who can remember."

"And in all that time it's always been just friends?" Lisa asked. "I mean, it's never progressed to anything more serious?"

Jess shook her head. "I know it must sound strange, but that's how it's always been. I've known him so long he feels more like a brother to me. To get romantic now would be . . ." Jess pretended to shiver. "Like being romantic with your *brother*."

"Yuck." Lisa wrinkled her nose.

"You must have a brother," Jess said.

"I do," said Lisa. "He's thirteen and the thought of him being romantic with any girl is totally gross."

They laughed.

On the other side of town, back on the beach road and a few miles from the lifeguard shack, Reed steered his jeep through a tall, black wrought-iron gate. Then he drove down a long gravel driveway lined on both sides by tall maples that formed an arch over the driveway. To the right was a broad green perfectly manicured lawn and several flower gardens. To the left was a tennis court bracketed by a tall fence covered with vines. Ahead was a circular driveway with a white marble fountain at its center. Beyond the driveway stood a large redbrick mansion with stately white columns and yellow and green window awnings. If someone walked in the front door of the mansion, past the stately living room and out through the back door, he would find himself overlooking a broad slate patio, a large blue swimming pool, and beyond that, the beach and ocean.

The Petersens' estate was called Breezes.

Reed pulled up around the top of the circular driveway and stopped. In the passenger seat, his brother Billy leaned forward and crushed out his cigarette in the car's ashtray. Billy had a jeep of his own that matched Reed's, but it was in the shop being repaired after the last of his frequent fender benders.

Reed watched as his brother started to push open the door on his side of the jeep. He knew that if he didn't say something now, he wouldn't have a chance for the rest of the night. Once inside, Billy would go up to his room and lock the door and spend the night with his CD player, his computer, and video equipment. Or he might go outside and drink beer alone on the beach while he tried to shoot sea gulls with his pellet gun. Either way, he wouldn't want Reed around.

"Congratulations, Billy," Reed said.

Billy turned and squinted at him. "For what?"

"Making senior guard."

"Like you care," Billy said with a smirk.

Reed was never sure what to say to his brother.

Billy was always so angry, so filled with rage. He could never accept anything Reed said without immediately suspecting some ulterior motive.

"I do care," Reed said. "Why don't you believe me?"

Billy stared back at him and a nasty smile curled onto his lips. "Congratulations to you, too."

"To me?" Reed was puzzled.

"Yeah. That rookie partner you've got is a real babe. Too bad you don't have much time."

"Until what?" Reed asked. Sometimes it seemed as if Billy spoke in riddles.

"Until Paula gets back from Mexico or wherever she is," his brother said. "Now that you've got that honey on the chair with you, I'll bet you're really sorry Paula is coming back."

Reed just stared back at his brother. "Okay, so Jess Sloat is a pretty girl. She and I happen to be in the busiest chair on the beach."

"Yeah, I know," Billy snickered. "The lives of too many people depend on you two being able to work well together. You can't afford any emotional complications. And blah blah blah."

What Billy said was true. Reed couldn't understand why his brother would make light of it. "What's with you?"

Billy didn't reply. He just smirked and headed through the broad white front door and into the mansion. Reed stayed behind in the jeep and watched. The funny thing was, his brother was right — Reed was *not* looking forward to Paula's return.

FIVE

After two weeks on the job, Jess could look back and feel satisfied knowing that things had gone surprisingly well. The weather had been good and the waves about average for that time of year. The most serious injury she'd taken care of had been an ankle twisted during a Frisbee football game. She and Reed had whistled plenty of warnings to swimmers who went out too far or swam too close to restricted areas, but they had not had to make a single rescue. That was what preventive lifeguarding was all about.

Her feelings about Reed Petersen were not as clear. As the week progressed, he stopped testing her, gave her fewer and fewer orders, and seemed to rely more on her own ability to judge which situations needed attention and which didn't. Jess kept waiting for him to use the position of senior lifeguard to his advantage in some way, but he was consistently fair and considerate to everyone he dealt with, including a few rowdy people who didn't deserve much consideration at all.

While some of the other senior guards used their rookies as gofers to get them drinks and food from the snack bar, Reed always went by himself, and always asked Jess if she needed anything. He didn't even cut in on the snack bar line. Lifeguards were allowed to cut to the front so that they could get what they needed quickly and get back out to their jobs. Instead, Reed always made sure Jess had backup help, and then stood in line like everyone else.

"It's just part of the act," Andy said when she asked him about things Reed did. But Jess wasn't so sure.

The way he treated girls also puzzled her. Being so good-looking, Reed was the target of constant attention from the younger girls who hung around the lifeguard stand chattering and giggling and trying to catch his eye. All week, Reed had been polite but firm with them, and he never once gave in to the temptation of basking in their adulation. He acted the same way toward the older girls and even some admiring women who looked as if they were in their *twenties*. Jess could only assume that he was just being faithful to Paula.

As the second week of lifeguarding began, Jess

found herself wondering what Paula was like. She'd heard Andy's opinion, but, after all, Andy was decidedly anti-rich city kids. Could he be as wrong about Reed's girlfriend as he appeared to be about Reed?

"Is this Reed Petersen's chair?" a voice asked.

Jess looked down at a dark-haired girl wearing an almost microscopic red bikini. No doubt she was another of the almost constant stream of curious, admiring girls who heard about the handsome lifeguard in the Main chair. Unlike the other girls, however, this one had stepped over the rope barrier that separated the stand from the rest of the beach and was standing right at the base of the chair.

"Yes, but he had to go up to the lifeguard shack for a moment," Jess replied. Unlike the first week, when Reed would never leave Jess alone in the chair, this week he had begun to leave her for brief periods of time.

"So you're his new partner," the girl said.

"Yes, and I'm really sorry, but I'm not supposed to talk," Jess said, pointing to a large red-and-white sign on the stand that read:

FOR THE SAFETY OF OTHERS,
PLEASE DO NOT SPEAK TO
THE LIFEGUARDS

"You're not serious," the girl said.

Something about her tone of voice made Jess take another look. Besides the skimpy bikini, the girl was wearing a thick gold necklace, several gold bracelets, and numerous rings. Her eyes were darkened with mascara and eye shadow, and her lips and nails were painted bright red.

Jess suddenly realized it had to be Paula.

"Yes, I am," Jess said. She was tempted to tell Paula that she wasn't supposed to come inside the rope that surrounded the stand. But that would only make Reed's girlfriend more antagonistic.

"Well, *excuuuse* me," Paula responded nastily. "You said he's in the lifeguard shack?"

Jess nodded and scanned the waters again, wondering why she felt so awkward knowing that Reed's girlfriend was there. Why should she care?

In the lifeguard shack, Reed watched as Hank started to unpack the Doppler radar from its large cardboard box.

"We've needed this kind of thing for a long time," Hank said.

"I'm glad the town sprang for it," Reed said. He glanced back out at the crowded beach, feeling uncomfortable about leaving his rookie partner out there alone. "Well, I'd better get back out there."

"Just one second," Hank said, looking up. "How're things going with Jess?"

"Pretty good," Reed said.

"She seems solid?"

Reed nodded.

"Whatever happened to the personality conflict?" Hank asked.

"Damned if I know." Reed smiled.

"So you're working well together?"

"I'd say so," Reed said. "She's got a good attitude. It seems like she takes it pretty seriously."

"Good, I'm glad."

Hank didn't appear to have anything more to say. As Reed turned to go, Paula suddenly popped into the doorway.

"Oh, Reed!" The next thing Reed knew, she'd thrown her arms around his neck. "I missed you so much!"

Caught by surprise, Reed glanced back at Hank, who smiled and winked.

"Paula, what are you doing here?" Reed sounded shocked. "I thought you weren't coming back for another week."

"I wasn't," Paula said. "But I missed you so much. I couldn't stay away."

*   *   *

That wasn't quite the truth. Since school ended, Paula had been having a blast on the Greek island of Corfu with Spiro, the twenty-three-year-old son of a shipping magnate. The idea that Reed was going to spend another summer sitting in that stupid lifeguard chair infuriated her. The thought of hanging around that stupid beach every day just to be near him made her ill. She'd never understood why Reed wanted to be a lifeguard anyway. It was such a . . . a menial kind of job, especially for someone who didn't need a job at all.

Even though Paula was having fun playing with Spiro on his father's 150-foot motor yacht, it was still her habit, early every Sunday morning, to call Far Hampton, where it was still Saturday night, and speak to Reed. It wasn't so much that she missed Reed as it was to make sure he wasn't going out with other girls. The past Saturday night Billy had answered the phone and mentioned something about Reed's beautiful new lifeguarding partner. As quick as you could say olive oil, Paula told Spiro there was a family crisis at home and started packing her bags to catch the next flight back to the States.

"Did you miss me as much as I missed you?" Paula asked, pressing herself against him.

"What do you think?" Reed replied. The truth was, he'd found he'd enjoyed the last few weeks without her.

"I think you missed me a lot," Paula said, although it hardly mattered. Now that she was back, she was going to stick to him like glue until she established whether that pretty blonde in the lifeguard chair was any kind of a threat.

"Hey, Paula, want to see something great?" Hank asked, holding up a large round metal disc that looked like an oversized wok. "It's the antenna for our new Doppler radar."

Paula pretended to be interested as Hank explained how the radar would detect fast-developing thunderstorm cells. Then it was time for Reed to head back to the lifeguard stand.

"It'd be great to have something like that on *Simplicity*," Reed said as he and Paula walked back across the hot sand to the Main chair. "It would make the chance of getting caught in a sudden storm a lot less likely."

"Maybe you should look into getting one," Paula said. Actually, she dreaded the thought of anything that might make Reed want to sail more. She hated sailing. It was boring, the rocking back and forth nauseated her, and she was always chipping nails in her efforts to hold on. It wasn't the same as Spiro's yacht, which always stayed anchored in a bay and had a staff of five.

"Naw, it's too expensive," Reed said.

"Reed . . ." Paula looked at him in amazement.

"You know I hate to take money from my father," Reed said. "He pays for school and that's enough."

Reed had the strangest attitude toward money of any rich person Paula had ever known. He actually insisted on earning almost every penny he spent. Actually, that was one attribute Paula didn't mind. She looked forward to the day they would be married, thus bringing the future ownership of the Petersen-Lewis Land Development Corporation under one roof. If Reed didn't like to spend money, she'd more than make up for that.

"So how's it going this year?" Paula asked.

"Not bad," Reed said.

"I see you've got a new partner," she said, watching carefully for his reaction.

"Jess? Yes, she's a rookie."

"I forget how it works," Paula said. "Do you keep the same partner all summer long?"

"Usually," Reed answered. Ahead in the water, something caught his eye and he began to walk faster.

"Reed, what is it?" Paula asked.

"I'm not sure yet," Reed answered and left her as he sprinted ahead.

Jess was standing on the lifeguard stand, a pair of binoculars pressed against her eyes. About fifty yards offshore, a large patch of water appeared to be boiling. She heard the wooden ladder of the lifeguard stand creak as Reed quickly climbed up beside her.

"Jess, you see it?"

"I've been watching it for a couple of minutes," Jess said, handing the binoculars to him.

"What do you think?" Reed asked.

"Definitely a school of bluefish feeding on the surface," Jess said. "The question is, are they moving inshore or staying off?"

Reed reached for the binoculars. While bluefish couldn't be considered a threat to life, they had razor-sharp teeth and had been known to inflict ghastly wounds on swimmers caught in the middle of a feeding frenzy.

"I don't think we can take a chance," Reed said. "Start clearing the water. I'll call Hank and the other chairs."

A second later, Jess was blowing her whistle as hard as she could and shouting at people to leave the water immediately. Each chair had its own phone with a direct line to the lifeguard shack and the other chairs. Reed got on it and warned the other guards.

Suddenly Jess saw something that sent a chill down her spine. The feeding school had taken a sharp turn toward shore.

"It's coming in, Reed!" she shouted.

Reed looked up and saw that she was right. And there were still some swimmers and boogie boarders out in the water. In a flash he stepped to the edge of the lifeguard stand and jumped ten feet to the sand below. Without pausing, Jess followed, but her landing was a lot harder than she'd expected and she stumbled forward.

"Look out, Reed!"

Reed spun around and caught Jess just as she was about to tumble into him. Suddenly she was in his arms. She could feel his taut muscles supporting her and his heart beating hard in his chest. His skin felt warm and smooth. For a split second their eyes locked.

"You okay?" Reed let go and stepped back.

"Yes, uh, thanks."

But Reed was already turning back toward the water. "Come on!"

Together they ran down to the surf, blowing

their whistles and waving as they shouted at the laggards still in the water to head for shore immediately.

Meanwhile, back up the beach, Paula watched all the activity with a look of disdain. She couldn't *believe* the move that "rookie" Jess had made, pretending to lose her balance and stumble into Reed's arms. Of all the obvious, transparent tricks! One thing was for sure, Jess was no rookie when it came to putting the moves on guys. And then, in the few short moments that followed, Reed and she had acted more like a team than Paula and Reed ever had. Paula pressed her lips together and squinted angrily. This was definitely a situation that required close monitoring.

SIX

With the exception of Gary Pilot, who of course gave them an argument about having to leave the water, the whole operation had gone quickly and efficiently. Everyone had stayed out of the water until the school of bluefish had disappeared. Then the lifeguards blew their whistles, indicating that it was okay to swim again.

Panting for breath from the sudden excitement, Reed and Jess climbed back into the chair. Reed's heart was still pounding. He always found it difficult to settle back into the chair after something so intense. He noticed that next to him, Jess swept her pretty blonde hair back with her hand and used her arm to wipe a few beads of perspiration off her forehead. He felt as if he should say something, but he wasn't sure what.

Finally, he held out his hand. "Way to go, partner."

Jess grinned and slapped it. "Thanks."

For a moment they both smiled at each other. Then Reed remembered where he was and turned back to watch the patrons and the water. A few dozen yards offshore a black-headed tern suddenly banked out of the air and crashed straight down into the water, probably for a morsel of bait left behind by the marauding blue-fish. Something had changed between him and his partner, but he couldn't quite tell what it was. All he knew was that when he thought back to all the excitement that had taken place, the moment that stood out was when he'd held her in his arms.

The rest of the afternoon couldn't pass fast enough for Jess. Her insides were a tumult of mixed feelings and emotions. Like some mysterious recipe, it was very hard to figure out what all the different ingredients were. She felt exalted at successfully handling her first crisis, and proud that Reed had complimented her.

But her feelings about Reed were harder to identify. She felt a vague sense of discomfort. Something wasn't going the way it was supposed to, something that concerned her partner. She fought the temptation to glance across at Reed again. Inside she felt a sense of admiration and warmth toward him. The problem was, it wasn't purely professional.

At the end of the day, as she headed back toward the lifeguard shack to sign out, Jess noticed that Paula was waiting on the porch. Jess forced a smile on her face, but Paula didn't bother to respond in kind.

"Nice move before," she said.

"I'm sorry?" Jess stopped on the porch and stared at her.

"You heard me." Paula arched a finely plucked eyebrow.

"What are you talking about?" Jess asked, although deep inside she had a feeling she knew what Paula was referring to.

"Falling into Reed's arms," Paula said. "Very neatly done."

"It was an accident," Jess said flatly.

Paula gave an exaggerated nod. "Oh, sure."

"Oh, sure is right." Jess turned to continue into the shack, but Paula blocked her way.

"Your father's the police chief, isn't he?" Paula had spent the afternoon doing her homework.

"So?"

"You're sort of a local girl," Paula said. "On your father's salary I bet you don't get to travel much."

Jess had had enough of Paula's insults. "What's your point?"

"My point is that for some reason my boyfriend Reed insists on doing this stupid lifeguarding job, and you were lucky enough to be picked as his partner," Paula said. "Just don't fall into the trap of thinking that just because you're both lifeguards you two have a lot in common . . . because you don't."

"Why don't you just drop — " Before Jess could finish the sentence, Reed stepped out of the lifeguard shack. He looked surprised to find them both standing there. Jess glared at him angrily, then stormed past him and into the shack.

Reed frowned and turned to Paula. "What was that all about?"

"I haven't the slightest idea." Paula gave him an innocent smile and then slid her arm through his.

"Earth to Jess," Lisa said.

Jess blinked and looked up at her. As usual, Lisa was wearing her worn denim jacket with the rose on the back. Under it she wore a black Danskin top and black leggings with lace at the bottoms. It was about nine o'clock in the evening and they were sitting in Rafe's ice-cream parlor. Lisa had called around dinnertime and asked if she wanted to go out. Jess had been in a terrible mood and almost said no, but then decided that getting out might be just what she needed. As usual, Jess felt most comfortable in a plain white blouse and comfortably worn old jeans.

Rafe's had once been a hole in the wall with a sticky red counter, a couple of rickety stools, and a ceiling fan, but then the tourists and city people had discovered it and the owner had the place redone. Now there were shiny wood-paneled walls, fancy booths with colorful Tiffany-style lamps, air conditioning, and a wide variety of low-fat and no-fat ice-cream substitutes for sale at ridiculous prices.

"Where were you just now?" Lisa asked.

"Here," Jess said.

"Look at your ice cream."

Jess looked down. Her cup of frozen vanilla yogurt with chocolate sprinkles was half melted.

"You haven't touched it," Lisa said. "You've been staring out that window like you thought Luke Perry was going to walk by."

"You never know," Jess said with a smile. "In this town he might."

"It really changes in the summer, doesn't it?" Lisa said.

"And how." Jess nodded and ate a spoonful of semi-melted yogurt.

A small tin bell rang as the door opened and three guys stepped in, talking loudly about a baseball game. They were all tall and good-looking and were dressed in khaki pants, polo shirts, and deck shoes. Two of them had white sweatshirts with *St. Peter's Lacrosse* stenciled across the chest draped over their shoulders. As they passed Jess and Lisa, they smiled.

"Do you know what St. Peter's is?" Lisa whispered, leaning across the table.

"A school?" Jess guessed. She'd seen guys around town wearing those sweatshirts before.

"The coolest prep school going," Lisa said. "A lot of city kids go there." She paused for a moment to watch the three boys and then turned to Jess. "Have you ever dated any guys from the city?"

"Not really." Jess started to shake her head, but even as she did, Reed Petersen's face popped into her thoughts.

"Neither have I," Lisa said. "Of course, before I moved here, I never met any."

"You've met them here?" Jess asked, surprised.

"Well, no." Lisa grinned. "But I mean, at least they're around. It raises the possibility."

Until recently Jess might have said she'd never date a guy from the city. But tonight she didn't.

"Why is dating a guy from the city any different from dating someone who lives around here?" she asked.

"Oh, I don't know." Lisa grinned. "I guess I think of them as being more sophisticated. And some of them definitely have more money and drive better cars."

"Does that mean you'd prefer to date a guy from the city?" Jess asked.

"I don't know." Lisa gazed back at the three guys ordering at the counter. "I guess it still depends on the guy. You know, it's like around here. Some guys are nice and some guys aren't so nice. I'll bet it's the same with guys from the city."

Jess wondered if it was true. Could Reed Petersen be a nice guy? He'd been thoughtful to her as her senior guard, but could anyone who dated a witch like Paula really be nice? It didn't make sense.

"Have you ever had a serious relationship?" Lisa asked.

Jess shook her head. "Not really."

"How come?"

"I don't know. I guess I haven't met the right person." Again, the memory of being in Reed's arms came back to her. *Stop it!* she wanted to shout at herself. If any guy should have been completely off-limits, it was Reed.

"I know what you mean," Lisa said. "I have the most incredible record of meeting the wrong people."

"What do you mean?" Jess asked.

"I mean, every time I decide to like a guy, he either likes someone else or just doesn't like me. It never fails."

Just then a familiar face passed the window and glanced in.

"It's Andy!" Lisa waved excitedly.

Andy grinned and came in. He was wearing a white T-shirt with a hole at the neck and a faded stain in front, a pair of cutoff blue jeans, and old dirty tennis shoes.

"Hey, Lisa," he said, sitting down beside her and facing Jess. "Hi, Jess, how's it going?"

"Pretty good," Jess said. "Where were you today?" She hadn't seen him at the beach.

"I had the day off," Andy said. He pointed to Jess's yogurt. "It's melting."

"You can have it," Jess said.

"All right!" Andy dug in.

"How's it going in the chair with Billy?" Lisa asked.

"Got a couple of hours?" Andy shook his head.

"Just the headlines, please," Jess said.

"The guy's totally obnoxious," Andy said. "You know how we're supposed to be looking for patroons in trouble?"

"Patroons?" Lisa repeated with a laugh.

"That's Andy-talk for the patrons," Jess explained.

"So I mean, looking out for them is basically our job, right?" Andy continued. "Well, about ten times a day he orders me to look out for Hank so he can grab a smoke and not get caught."

"You really ought to tell Hank," Jess said.

"I told you, Jess," Andy said. "If Billy ever found out I squealed on him, my life wouldn't be worth a spoonful of melted yogurt."

Jess nodded, but found herself thinking how different Reed was. Meanwhile, the three guys from St. Peter's sat down in a booth. Andy suddenly grew quiet and stared at them.

"So how are things with Reed?" Lisa asked Jess.

"Okay, I guess." Jess shrugged, aware that Andy had turned back and was studying her curiously.

"Did you hear about the bluefish?" Lisa asked Andy.

Andy shook his head.

"A school came really close to shore," Lisa said. "Jess and Reed did a great job of clearing the water."

"Thanks," Jess said.

"So, you two are working well together?" Andy raised an eyebrow.

"I guess. He doesn't say much, except about lifeguarding."

Andy shook his head. "Weird guy."

"Why?" Jess asked.

"Just stuff Billy says."

"Like what?" Jess asked.

"How come you're so interested?" Andy sounded annoyed.

"I'm not really," Jess said, suddenly on the defensive. "But I do sit with him every day, so I'm curious." She pretended to ignore the boys in the booth who were glancing at her and talking in low voices.

"Billy says Reed won't take any money from his father," Andy said. "Like the guy's got millions, but he insists on earning every penny he spends. Billy says it's this holier-than-thou attitude his brother has."

"It sounds like Reed and Billy don't get along too well," Lisa said.

"You're telling me," Andy replied.

"So what would you do if you had millions, Andy?" Lisa asked.

"Spend it," Andy said with a grin.

"How?" Jess asked.

"I'd probably party with my closest friends for about a year. And whenever it got boring I'd rent an airplane so we could move the party someplace else and make it fun again."

"And then what?" Lisa asked.

"I don't know," Andy said. "I'd probably get out of Far Hampton."

"What's wrong with Far Hampton?" Lisa asked.

"It's boring," Andy said. "I mean, except for the summer, the place is dead nine months of the year."

"Andy's going to be a lawyer someday," Jess said.

"You can't be a lawyer in Far Hampton?" Lisa asked.

"Sure you can," Andy said. "You'll just spend your life doing DWI cases."

"DWI?" Lisa frowned.

"Driving While Intoxicated," Jess said.

"It's a major local pastime," Andy said. "I figure once I get out of law school, I'll go to work for one of those firms in the city. That's where the action is."

"Uh, excuse me," a voice said. Jess and her friends looked up into the face of a tall, good-looking blond guy, one of the three city kids from the other booth.

"Yes?" Andy said, but the guy ignored him and stared at Jess.

"You're not from around here, right?" he said.

"Yes, I am," Jess replied.

The guy grinned and turned back to his two friends. "See, I *told* you."

"Ask how long," one of the other guys said.

"Why do you want to know?" Andy asked.

"We had a bet," the guy explained. "They said she was too good-looking to come from around here." He looked at Jess again. "You didn't just move or anything?"

Jess shook her head. "No, I've lived here my whole life."

The guy turned to his friends again. "See?"

"Then ask her if she's available," one of his friends yelled.

"Why don't you guys go back to the city where you belong?" Andy said angrily.

"Ooooh, we're scared." The guys in the booth laughed.

Suddenly Andy rose halfway out of his seat

and waved a fist at them. "You want to make something of it?"

"Andy, sit down," Jess said firmly and put her hand on his shoulder. There were three of them and only one Andy. It was clear to Jess that Andy couldn't win.

"No," Andy said, shaking her off.

"I'd listen to her," the tall blond guy said, threateningly.

"Make me," Andy dared him.

The situation was tense. The other two guys in the booth were starting to get up to join their friend in case a fight broke out. Jess was worried they'd really beat Andy up.

It was Lisa who came to the rescue. "She's a good friend of Reed Petersen's, you know."

The tall blond guy looked surprised. "You know Reed?"

Jess nodded.

"We all do," Lisa said.

"Bull," one of the guys said.

"It's true," Lisa said. "We're all town lifeguards with him."

"Give me a break," one of the guys said. "Reed Petersen, a *town* lifeguard?"

"She's right," the blond guy said. "That's what he does in the summer." Then he turned to Andy. "You're lucky you know Reed, but next time I wouldn't push it." He waved to his friends. "Come on, guys, let's get out of here before the chip on this guy's shoulder grows any bigger."

The three guys left. Andy sat down.

"Those city guys are all chicken," he said.

"Why did you have to get involved with them?" Jess asked.

"Me?" Andy asked, surprised. "They're the ones who made that dumb bet."

"So, they were just being stupid," Jess said. "You didn't have to start a fight."

Andy shrugged. "I just don't like that kind of stuff. It's their attitude. Like no one from around here could be good enough for them. I've heard them talk. They think all the guys around here are stupid and all the girls are tramps. This used to be a fun place until they started hanging around."

Jess turned to Lisa. "How'd you know they'd know Reed?"

"He's got a big St. Peter's bumper sticker on the back of his jeep," Lisa explained. "I noticed it the other day."

Jess studied her. "I didn't know you had such sharp eyes."

Lisa smiled sheepishly.

Andy finished Jess's yogurt. "So what do you say we get out of here before any more of those jerks show up?"

Jess and Lisa nodded in agreement.

A block away, Paula was window shopping with Reed in tow. In the summer, many of Far Hampton's chic boutiques stayed open until ten o'clock, hoping to attract tourists after dinner. Reed had just waited fifteen minutes in a store called Attractions while Paula tried on a tight-fitting yellow party dress with black polka dots.

"Can you believe they want seven hundred and fifty dollars for that dress?" Paula said as they left the store and stepped out onto the side-walk. "I tried the same dress on at Saks and they only wanted six hundred for it."

Reed stopped and stared at her. "Wait just a minute — you already tried that dress on at Saks?"

"Sure." Paula nodded.

"Then why did you have to try it on again?"

"Well, they wanted more money, so I thought there might be something better about it," Paula explained.

Two doors down was another boutique. Paula

started to drag him inside, but Reed had been inside enough stores that evening.

"I think I'll walk down to Village Electronics," he said.

"Just don't get lost," Paula said and went inside.

"I won't," Reed said, although the temptation to get lost was definitely there. He just didn't feel as if he and Paula had anything in common anymore. Sometimes he wondered if they even spoke the same language. They'd liked each other a lot when they first met after sixth grade, the year his father, Charles Petersen, had merged Petersen Land Development Corporation with Lewis Real Estate, which was owned by Paula's father.

In junior high they'd gone on skiing trips to Utah and Colorado together, and sailed in the Caribbean, but more recently Paula had started to make excuses not to go sailing or skiing. All she seemed to want to do was shop and go to parties and fancy restaurants. Reed had gone in the opposite direction, growing bored with parties and restaurants, and preferring to be out of doors as much as possible.

As Reed strolled along the sidewalk, in and out of the shadows caused by the streetlights and trees, he found himself fantasizing about breaking up with Paula. It was a fantasy he'd had a lot lately, but he worried that it might cause unpleasant repercussions between his father and Bernard Lewis. So for now he decided to simply make up a lot of excuses for not seeing Paula as much as he used to.

After Rafe's, Lisa and Andy decided to stop in a card shop. Jess stayed outside on the sidewalk. The night air was cool and filled with the scent of trees in bloom. And there, strolling down the dimly lit sidewalk, lost in thought, was Reed Petersen.

"Uh, hi, Reed," she said.

Despite the darkness, she could see that Reed looked startled to see her. "Oh, uh, hello, Jess. What are you doing here?"

Jess smiled, covering the sudden nervous feeling inside. "The same thing you're doing, I guess."

"Paula's in a store." Reed pointed back down the block.

"Andy and Lisa are in a store," Jess said, pointing in the direction she'd just come from.

"How come you're not with them?" Reed asked.

"Maybe for the same reason you're not with Paula," Jess said.

"I wanted to look in this window," Reed said, pointing at the window of Village Electronics. Jess looked in. It was a store she'd never really paid attention to. Although the store was closed, the display cases were lit and inside she could see all sorts of cameras and phones and tape players. For a moment they both stared at the window. Then Jess noticed that instead of looking at all the gear, Reed was staring at her reflection.

"Is there something you need?" Jess asked, looking back at his reflection.

Reed found it difficult to tear his eyes away from her reflection in the window. It was true that they'd been sitting together in the Main chair for more than two weeks, but they rarely had a chance to look at each other. Though he'd been raised not to stare, he couldn't get enough of her, and found himself stealing glances at every opportunity. There was just something about the openness of her face, and the liveliness of her eyes — not to mention her beauty — that made him want to drink her up.

But she'd asked him a question and he hadn't answered it.

"Actually, there isn't," he said. "I'd just rather be outside than in a store. There's something about the night air."

"After a hot day at the beach it feels refresh-ing," Jess said.

Once again Reed just stared at her.

"Is something wrong?" Jess asked.

"Oh, uh, no." Reed tore his eyes away from her. "I, uh, guess I'm not used to seeing you in clothes."

"Huh?" Jess looked surprised.

Reed grinned. "You're always in a bathing suit at the beach."

"I thought guys preferred that," Jess teased.

"Well, I guess they do."

"You sound like you're not certain."

"Maybe it depends on what you're used to," Reed said. "I'm not used to seeing you in jeans. It's sort of a new you."

"The new me in old jeans," Jess said.

Reed smiled and glanced out at the street. "So, do you take a lot of walks at night?"

"Sometimes," Jess said. "But it's the kind of thing I sometimes forget about."

"I know what you mean," Reed said. "I like walking along the beach at night, but each sum-mer I forget how much I like it until I do it again."

Jess imagined walking along the beach with Reed, with the full moon out and the waves crashing. But when she imagined him slipping his arm around her waist, she shook herself out of the dream. No, that's not what she wanted.

"So, uh, have you done it yet this summer?" she asked.

"No." Reed turned and looked into her eyes and smiled. "How about you?"

Jess shook her head. The memory of that afternoon at the beach flooded back into her thoughts. The feeling of his warm skin and his strong arms around her, enveloping and steadying her. Other boys had put their arms around her, and yet none had made her feel the way Reed had. What she'd felt with Reed was something new and more powerful than she'd ever felt before. It wasn't that silly, giggly experimenting with the opposite sex. It was magnetic, almost too strong, and certainly more serious and grown-up than anything she'd felt before. It both frightened her and made her yearn to have it again.

No! Stop! She had to stop herself from thinking about it. He was Reed Petersen, rich city boy who would be going back to St. Peter's in the fall. It was simply out of the question.

"I thought we worked well today," Reed said.

"Me, too." Jess wondered why he'd said that. Was he remembering the same things she was? Was he feeling them, too?

Stop it, Jess!

"I guess the real test will be your first rescue," Reed said.

The thought sent a shiver through Jess.

"It scares me," she suddenly blurted out. Immediately she was angry with herself. Hank had stressed how important it was to appear confident. Why had she admitted she was scared? Especially to *him!*

"It scares everyone," Reed said. "Even after you've done it a dozen times."

"Is that how many times you've rescued people?" Jess asked.

"Probably," Reed said with a chuckle.

"Is this a chance meeting?" someone asked.

Jess recognized the voice. It was Paula, coming toward them carrying a shopping bag.

"Jess left her friends in the card store and went for a walk," Reed said. "We just ran into each other."

"Oh, sure," Paula said in a voice that indicated she didn't believe it was a coincidence for a second. She slid her arm through Reed's. "But how lucky for you. You probably have so much to talk about after your exciting day saving people from *bluefish!*"

Paula's words reeked of vicious sarcasm.

"Hey, Jess!"

Jess turned around and saw Lisa and Andy coming toward them. Their pace slowed when they saw who she was with.

"Oh, uh, hi, Reed," Andy said.

Reed said hello and introduced Paula to Jess's friends. "Paula, this is Andy Moncure and Lisa Jones, two of the lifeguards."

"What luck," Paula said. "It's a lifeguard reunion!"

"Well, we'd better get going," Jess said, eager to leave before Paula had an opportunity to sink her claws in any deeper. "It was nice to see you, Reed, and you, too, Paula."

"Oh, yes," Paula replied. "Lovely to see you, too, Jess." She abruptly steered Reed in the opposite direction down the sidewalk. It seemed to Jess that Paula wanted to get Reed away from them as fast as she could.

Meanwhile, Jess, Andy, and Lisa strolled down the dark sidewalk toward Lisa's VW.

"What was that all about?" Andy asked.

"Nothing," Jess said. "We just happened to run into each other."

"Isn't Paula something?" Lisa asked.

"Yes," Jess said. "She sure is."

SEVEN

The next day Andy trudged up the beach toward the snack stand. It was the third time that morning that Billy had sent him to fetch something and it wasn't even lunchtime yet! The problem was a couple of girls had started hanging around the East Wing chair, probably because Billy was a Petersen and they didn't know what a jerk he was. This just made Billy more of a jerk than ever. Now he had to show off by constantly sending Andy on errands.

This time he'd sent Andy to get a frozen Milky Way. Andy wished he could unwrap it and fill it with sand and rewrap it. He could just picture Billy sitting up on the chair with all the girls around, biting into a nice sandy candy bar.

"Oh, hi," someone said.

Andy looked up and found himself facing Paula, Reed Petersen's girlfriend, wearing a bikini that showed so much bare skin it should have been illegal.

"Uh, hi."

"I met you last night, didn't I?" Paula said.

Andy nodded warily. He'd heard about how stuck-up and snobby she was.

"Can I ask you a question?" Paula asked.

"Okay," Andy said.

"I've noticed you keep making trips to the snack stand," Paula said innocently. "I thought Reed said you were a lifeguard."

"I am," Andy said, "but Billy Petersen's my senior guard and he keeps sending me on errands."

"Is he supposed to do that?" Paula asked.

"Well, once in a while, maybe," Andy said.

"But not three times in one morning," Paula said.

Andy nodded, glad someone noticed. Maybe Paula wasn't as bad as Jess and Lisa said. Well, not that it mattered. He really didn't have time to stand around and talk to her.

"I guess I'd better get back to the chair," he said, and started around her.

"So not only does he make you his gofer, but he says you have to hurry?" Paula asked.

Andy suddenly stopped. She was right. Why

should he rush for Billy? "No, I don't have to hurry."

"Oh, good," Paula said, "because there's something I want to show you. I'm really scared of it."

On this beach? Andy thought. But Paula reached for his hand and squeezed it tightly.

"It's by my towel," Paula said. "I don't know what it is."

The next thing Andy knew, Paula was leading him by the hand down toward her towel on the part of the beach covered by the Main chair. Paula's spot was marked by a luxurious bright red towel, a portable bright yellow CD player, several bottles of suntan oil, and a small pile of glossy fashion magazines.

"Here, this is it," Paula said, pointing to the sand. "I really don't know what it is, but it looks like it could sting someone."

Something greenish–brown and pointy was sticking up out of the sand. Andy thought he knew what it was. He reached down and pulled it out.

"It's nothing to worry about," he said. "Just a tail from a dead horseshoe crab."

"Oh, you're so brave!" Paula gasped and slid her hands around his biceps.

"Naw, it's nothing," Andy said. "I've seen a

million of them. I'll just throw it in the garbage
for you."

"Would you?" Paula leaned forward and
kissed him on the cheek, while making sure she
rubbed against his arm. "You're such a dear."

Andy beamed. After all, it wasn't every day
that a girl as hot-looking as Paula kissed him.
And she was Reed Petersen's girlfriend, too.

"Hey, if I go find another one, will you kiss
me again?" he asked.

"You never know," Paula said with a wink.

Paula watched Andy walk away, looking two
inches taller than he had a few minutes ago.
Throughout the whole scene she had kept one
eye on the Main chair, hoping Reed would turn
around and see her with Andy. But if he had,
he gave no sign of it. Damn! she thought. She'd
worked so hard on orchestrating the whole
thing, from watching Andy make those treks
across the sand to burying that stupid crab tail
in the sand. Now it seemed as if it was all for
nothing.

Paula sat down on her towel and stared up at
Reed. There was definitely something wrong
with him. He hardly paid any attention to her
anymore and almost seemed bored when they
were together. Jess Sloat was involved somehow.

It couldn't be a coincidence that just as Reed started sitting with her his interest in Paula appeared to be on the wane. It was time to get him interested again, and if trying to use Andy to make him jealous didn't work, Paula was just going to have to come up with something more drastic.

It was Jess who spotted the potential first.

"Reed," she said, pointing at something round and white bobbing in the water beyond the breaking waves, "there's someone out there."

Reed stood in the chair and cupped his hands over his eyes to get a better look. "Go get her, Jess. Take the torp."

Jess looked at Reed with wide eyes. "It's only my second week."

"You can do it."

"Are you sure?"

Reed nodded.

Jess felt a rush of adrenaline as she leapt off the chair, grabbed the torpedo buoy, and ran into the surf. There was no time to think now. She had to get to that swimmer before she disappeared from sight.

Fifty yards away in the water, Paula couldn't believe her eyes. Reed had sent Jess to rescue her!

The girl had less than two weeks' experience!

Well, one thing was for certain, there was no way Paula was going to wait around out there for Jess Sloat to rescue her. She started swimming in.

In the Main chair, Reed couldn't believe what *he* was seeing. One moment there was a swimmer floundering out beyond the breakers, the next moment she was swimming in using a confident, capable stroke. What was going on?

It was even more confusing for Jess, who didn't see Paula swim past her. Treading water in the waves, Jess lost sight of the victim. Had she gone down? Jess was terrified. There hadn't been a drowning at Far Hampton Beach in ten years!

She heard the shrill bleet of a whistle and turned to look. Back on shore, Reed was standing up in the chair, waving his right arm in a lazy half-circle — the all-clear signal. Jess still couldn't understand what had happened, but the signal meant she should come back in.

Paula couldn't afford to be caught. As she swam back toward the surf, she dove down under the surface and yanked the white bathing cap off her head. Then she joined a crowd of boys who were bodysurfing and rode in on a wave with them.

Reed climbed down from the chair. He wanted to talk to that swimmer. As he jogged toward the water, he saw the empty white bathing cap float to the surface. Now what? The whole situation was getting stranger and stranger. It was just by luck that he happened to glance to his right at a group of kids who'd bodysurfed a wave in. Paula! Reed couldn't believe it. Since when did Paula bodysurf?

Suddenly it began to make sense. Reed quickly waded into the surf, grabbed the bathing cap, and then waded out.

"Hey!" Reed shouted and walked up the beach toward Paula. His girlfriend had started to walk quickly away, slapping the side of her head with her open hand as if she had water in her ear and couldn't hear.

What an actress, Reed thought as he gained ground on her. Finally, when he was just a few feet behind her, he said, "Paula?"

Paula stopped and turned around, pretending to look surprised. "Oh, Reed, hi. What are you doing here?"

"Forget this?" Reed held out the bathing cap.

Paula frowned. "No. You know I never wear a bathing cap."

Reed smiled knowingly. "Right. And you never bodysurf, either. I guess it's just a day filled with firsts."

"What are you talking about?" Paula asked innocently.

"That was you out there pretending you needed a rescue," Reed said. "Sorry I messed up your plans by sending Jess."

Paula had learned a long time ago that there were three things you had to do when someone caught you lying. They were: (1) Deny (2) Deny and (3) Deny.

"I'm really not following you at all," Paula said. "Why would I pretend to need a rescue?"

Reed put his hands on his hips and shook his head angrily. "Just suppose there'd been someone else out there who really had needed help. We might have missed them."

"Why are you yelling at me?" Paula asked innocently.

"Damn it, Paula, you *know* why I'm yelling at you!" Reed yelled. "When are you going to quit playing these stupid games?"

"Reed, I really don't know what you're talking about," Paula claimed. "But I have to go dry off. Maybe we should talk again later when you've calmed down."

Reed watched her walk away. He knew Paula too well to think that he could ever get her to admit what she'd done. In Paula's peculiar code of ethics there was nothing wrong with lying. It was only a problem when you got caught.

A few moments later, Jess came out of the water, still wondering what had happened to the floundering swimmer and why Reed had waved her in. By now Reed had climbed back into the Main chair and Jess joined him.

"What happened to the swimmer?" she asked.

"She swam in," Reed said.

"But it looked like she was in trouble."

Reed nodded but didn't say anything.

"I don't get it," Jess said.

"Believe me, Jess," Reed said. "There's nothing to get."

Jess felt very puzzled. It was supposed to have been her first rescue, the biggest moment yet in her brief career as a lifeguard. Why was Reed pretending it had never happened?

"Was this another test?"

"Huh?" Reed looked surprised.

"You know," Jess said angrily. "Another one

of your little tests to make sure I'm good enough to sit in the Main chair with you."

Reed scowled at her. "What's with you?"

"What's with me?" Jess asked. "I just swam out there and couldn't find a victim. I thought she drowned. The next thing I know, you whistle me in and tell me nothing happened."

"That's right," Reed said.

"What's the big secret, Reed?" Jess asked hotly.

"It's not important," Reed replied tersely and turned to stare at the water.

Jess stared at him, amazed and hurt. Was it really not important, or was she not important enough to tell it to? Reed's was exactly the kind of haughty attitude she expected from city kids. Maybe she'd been wrong to think that he was any different.

A fire made of driftwood burned brightly on the beach that night, sending glowing ashes high into the clear, dark sky. The moon was almost full and moonlight sparkled on the ocean as smooth sets of waves crashed rhythmically against the shore. It was Friday and everyone had gotten paid that afternoon. A bunch of the lifeguards and their friends had decided to have a cookout on the beach. Jess, wearing an oversized man's sweatshirt with the sleeves rolled up and jeans, sat with Andy next to the fire while Lisa and some of the others threw a Day-Glo Frisbee on the beach.

"You're awful quiet tonight," Andy said.

Jess smiled weakly at him. He looked unusually handsome tonight, with the light and shadows of the fire dancing on his face. Jess had also noticed that he must have bought some new clothes that afternoon because tonight he was wearing khaki pants, a teal-blue polo shirt, and a white sweatshirt.

"Something wrong?" Andy asked.

Jess shook her head. She wanted to believe that nothing was wrong, that nothing could be wrong because Reed Petersen meant nothing to her. He was simply her senior guard. Other than that they had nothing in common, just as Paula had said. They would work together this summer. Then the fall would come and she'd go back to Far Hampton High while Reed went back to St. Peter's. Whatever she'd felt for Reed the previous day and night had been a mistake. No city boy would ever truly care about a girl from Far Hampton.

"Hey, Jess." Andy spoke softly and nudged her gently with his elbow. "Talk to me."

Jess looked at him and forced a smile onto her

face. She wished she could get her thoughts off Reed. Why was she thinking about him, anyway? He wasn't even there, and she could just about bet he wasn't thinking about her. He was probably at the Shore Club or some other fancy place, having a hot time with Paula.

"You look nice tonight, Andy," she said.

"You like these new duds?" Andy grinned. "Just got 'em this afternoon after work."

"You're starting to look more and more like a preppy from the city," she kidded him.

"Forget it." Andy shook his head. "It's not the clothes. It's what's inside."

"Whoa, looks like a party," someone behind them said.

Andy and Jess turned around. Behind them stood Gary Pilot and some of his friends. They were all about twelve or thirteen, all carrying boogie boards and wearing partial wetsuits. Even in the light of the fire, Jess could see that Gary's wetsuit was ripped and tattered.

"Hi, Gary," Jess said with a smile. "What's up?"

"We came down to do some night boogying," Gary said. "The waves look pretty awesome tonight."

"You know there's no swimming after dark," Jess said.

"Yeah, and like there's no jaywalking in town, either," Gary said, "but everyone does it."

"This is different," Jess said. "You could get hurt."

"And you don't think I could get hurt jaywalking?" Gary asked.

"All right, Gary!" "You tell her, dude!" "Highly excellent point!" His friends voiced their support. Gary smiled proudly.

Jess glanced at Andy, who just shrugged. "Let 'em surf if they want to," he said.

"See, even the other lifeguards think we should be allowed," Gary said.

Jess was disappointed that Andy didn't back her up, but it didn't matter.

"Gary, it's a bad idea," Jess said. "The town rule was created to protect people. If something happened out there, no one would see you."

"Hey, you're not even on duty," one of Gary's friends said. "We don't have to listen to you."

But Jess stood her ground. "Gary, I'm asking you not to do it."

"Don't listen to her, Gary," one of the other kids said.

"We're not going out that far," Gary said. "I don't see what the big deal is."

"You could get rolled by a wave," Jess said. "You could cramp up or have the wind knocked out of you and not be able to call for help. We can't see the rip currents at night. You could get caught in one and get pulled forty or fifty yards out."

"Sure," said one of Gary's friends. "And we could get hit by lightning, too."

The other guys chuckled.

Jess decided not to argue any longer. She had to do what she believed was right. She stood up and brushed the sand off her jeans. "Gary, if I have to call the police, I will."

Gary stared at her and then looked out at the dark waves crashing on the beach.

"You know what?" he said to his friends. "Those waves don't look so hot after all. I say we bag it for tonight and do something else."

"Aw, come on," one of his friends said. "Not after we dragged our stuff all the way down here."

Gary caught Jess's eye for a moment. They both knew he could have kept arguing, or even started surfing until the police arrived. To Jess, the look he gave her said, "Okay, I'll do you a favor this time, but you owe me one."

Then he turned back to his friends. "I say we bag it, guys. There's a new horror flick in town. Let's go see if we can sneak in."

The group of boogie boarders left. Jess

watched the boys start back up the beach. She couldn't help feeling proud that she'd been firm with Gary. She just wished Reed had been there to see it. She just wished Reed . . .

Wait! Why did she care about what Reed would think? Jess shook her head. She had to stop thinking about him.

"I'm impressed," Andy said. "I never thought they'd listen to you."

Jess looked down at her friend and smiled. If she had to stop thinking about Reed, maybe Andy could help. She reached down and offered her hand to help pull him up off the sand. "Come on, Andy. Let's take a walk."

EIGHT

Reed sat on the dock at Breezes and wiped the sweat off his brow. The heavy scent of wood varnish hung in the air around him. He'd just spent the last three hours varnishing *Simplicity*, the wooden-hulled, thirty-five-foot sloop his grandfather had left him. The boat required a lot of maintenance, but Reed didn't mind. He got a lot of pleasure sailing her.

"Going to the beach tonight?" Billy asked behind him.

Reed shook his head. "Wasn't planning on it."

"Then how about giving me a ride?" Billy asked. "My jeep's still in the shop."

Reed stood up and stretched. It was just like Billy not to talk to him for two days and then pop up asking for favors, but it was hard for Reed to say no. Billy was his brother. Maybe someday Billy would get over feeling so competitive and resentful, and they'd be able to be friends. Besides, it was too dark to do any more work on *Simplicity* tonight.

Together the brothers walked back across the broad lawn of the estate toward the garage.

"Going out with Paula tonight?" Billy asked.

"No," Reed replied. After the scene on the beach that afternoon, Reed was starting to feel like he'd had enough of Paula's games. He wasn't sure he cared anymore what effect their breaking up might have on their fathers' company. He wasn't sure he could stay with someone he no longer liked.

"What's with you two lately?" Billy asked. "You hardly spend any time together anymore."

Reed just shrugged. Even though Billy was his brother, some things were too personal to discuss.

Andy and Jess had gone for a long walk along the beach. They'd talked about how long they'd known each other and about all the fun times they'd had. Jess had sensed recently that Andy felt their relationship had changed. She could tell he was curious to see if they could go beyond being just friends. For several weeks she'd played it down, pretending not to take him seriously. Now she wondered if maybe she should. It made sense in so many ways. It was obvious they could get along. They knew each other's habits and quirks. A romantic relationship might just be the logical next step.

Stop trying to analyze it, she told herself. If it's going to happen, just let it happen.

Andy stopped walking and gazed up at the moon. They stood side by side, facing the ocean. Then he turned to her. The waves were crashing just a dozen yards away, sprinkling them with a light sea spray. Again Jess thought Andy looked handsome tonight. If only she wasn't taller than he was. . . .

"Jess," he said. "I know we've been friends for a long time . . . but . . . have you ever wondered what it might be like if things were different?"

"Yes," Jess replied.

"You have?" Andy sounded surprised.

Jess nodded.

"Wow, why didn't you ever tell me?"

Jess smiled and shrugged. "I guess it's not the kind of thing I felt comfortable talking about."

"But you do now?" Andy asked.

Jess could feel a sense of disappointment spreading through her. The answer to his question was, Not really. She didn't feel comfortable talking about it. It all felt too forced and unnatural. Maybe it would have been better if he'd said nothing and just took her in his arms. But Andy just stood there and stared at her as if she were a space alien or something.

"Andy, what is it?" Jess asked.

"I'm just totally surprised," he said.

"Why?"

"I . . . I guess I just always figured it was a hopeless dream," Andy said. "I mean, I thought it was about as likely as me suddenly growing another six inches and making the football team. It never occurred to me that you'd ever want me for more than just a friend."

"Maybe things change," Jess said, giving it one last shot.

"Wow, amazing." Andy just stood there staring at her with that silly expression on his face.

Jess stepped closer to him. "Let's not talk anymore."

"Right," Andy said, looking up at her. "No more talking. Not one more word. This is it, time to get serious."

They moved closer. Jess knew it felt all wrong. Why was she doing this? Because it would be great if it worked. Andy . . . good old Andy. . . .

"No more talking," Andy said, putting his hands around her waist.

"Andy . . ."

"I have to be quiet," he said. "This is romantic."

He leaned forward. Despite Jess's sense that it was all wrong, she stood there and let it happen. As if some miracle might turn . . .

What she thought next shocked her . . . *might turn Andy into Reed.*

It was supposed to be a kiss, but somehow they wound up with their foreheads touching.

"If Eskimos rub noses," Andy said, "maybe this is how pygmies kiss."

Jess sighed. It was wrong, all wrong. And not just because Andy couldn't be serious. She couldn't force romance to grow where it had never grown before.

They were still standing close together when they were suddenly caught in a set of headlights.

Reed hit the brakes and the jeep slid to a stop in the sand. For a split second, Jess and Andy stayed in their embrace, staring into the headlights like two startled deer.

Billy and Reed watched as they pulled away from each other.

"Too bad," Billy said quietly.

"What's too bad?" Reed asked.

"Looks like she's taken," Billy said.

Reed turned and stared at his brother. "*You* were interested?"

"In a hot-looking babe like that?" Billy said. "Who wouldn't be?"

Reed gunned the jeep's engine, sending a plume of sand high into the air as he started around the startled couple.

"Hey, what're you doing?" Billy said. "Slow down."

"Why?"

Billy grinned. "Maybe they need a ride."

"Maybe they want to be alone," Reed countered.

"Just slow down," Billy said.

They were only twenty feet away now. Reed slowed the jeep to a crawl on the sand and then stopped. He couldn't quite make out Jess's and Andy's expressions in the dark.

"Sorry," he said apologetically. "Didn't mean to interrupt."

Jess felt her face grow flushed. Fortunately she didn't think Reed could see it in the dark.

"You guys are pretty far from the fire," Billy said, looking mostly at Jess. "Want a ride back?"

Jess looked past Billy to Reed. Their eyes met, but his face remained inscrutable. Suddenly she didn't want to be way out on the beach alone with Andy.

"Okay," she said and the same moment Andy said, "No, thanks."

Jess and Andy turned and stared at each other.

"I thought . . ." Andy started to say.

Jess nodded, knowing precisely what he'd thought. But none of that seemed to matter now. He was her friend. He'd always been her friend, and it was silly to try and pretend they could be anything else except friends.

"Just climb in back," Billy said.

Jess climbed into the back of the jeep. Andy didn't move.

"Coming?" Billy asked.

Andy shook his head and stared straight at Jess. "No thanks, I feel like walking."

"Suit yourself," Billy said.

Reed put the jeep in gear and it lurched forward in four-wheel drive. Soon they were bouncing along over the sand. Jess looked back at Andy's silhouette growing smaller in the moonlight.

"So is this something new or something that's been going on for a while?" Billy asked, turning around in the front seat to look at her.

Jess caught Reed's eyes in the rearview mirror. His dark hair flew in the wind as he drove. She noticed that he was wearing an old paint-stained shirt.

"What are you talking about?" she asked.

"With Andy, my second-year guard," Billy said.

"We've been friends for a long time," she said.

"Friends?" Billy said. "It looked like more than that."

Again Jess's eyes met Reed's in the rearview. This time she felt that tingling sensation. Just like the night before.

"Look out!" Billy suddenly shouted.

Ahead Jess saw an old tree trunk illuminated in the headlights. Reed wrenched the steering wheel to the left and just barely missed hitting it.

"Hey," Billy said, grinning at his brother. "You ought to watch where you're going."

Reed glanced into the rearview once again and caught Jess's eye, then stared down the beach.

They arrived back at the fire, where the other guards had started roasting hot dogs. Jess noticed that a few of the guys were drinking beer. Billy hopped out of the front of the jeep and then offered his hand to help Jess climb out of the back. As Jess took it, she noticed that Reed stayed in the jeep.

"Want a beer?" Billy asked, still holding her hand and starting to pull her toward the fire.

"I think I'll pass, thanks," Jess said, pulling

back and letting her hand slide out of his. Billy looked disappointed, but Jess couldn't help that. She turned back to Reed just as he gunned the engine and put the jeep back in gear.

"Reed, wait," she said.

Reed stopped the jeep.

"You're going?" Jess asked. Jess had never been so forward in her life, but she didn't want to see him go.

Reed looked down the beach and then back at her.

"I was," he said.

"But," Jess added hopefully.

"I just changed my mind," Reed said with a smile.

The first person Andy saw when he returned from his walk along the beach was Billy Petersen, sitting alone staring at the waves with a can of beer in one hand and a cigarette in the other. Several empty beer cans were scattered in the sand around him.

"She went for a walk with my brother," Billy said and blew a smoke ring with well-practiced perfection.

"Jess?" Andy said, caught off guard.

"No, my aunt Tilly." Billy shook his head derisively.

Andy walked on toward the fire where the other guards and their friends were sitting in a circle. His buddy Donny, who worked as a waiter at the Shore Club, had arrived and Andy sat down beside him. Lisa was sitting across from them. She waved and Andy gave her a weak smile and then stared back at the flames. He didn't know what to think, except that he'd had a chance and had blown it. A few minutes ago, everything he'd ever hoped for had been right in his grasp and he'd been too nervous to follow through.

Next to him, Donny tapped him on the shoulder and pressed a cold, wet beer can into his hand.

"Have a cold brew, dude."

Andy stared down at the can in his hand. He felt incredibly disappointed and pissed off at himself. Maybe a couple of beers wasn't such a bad idea.

The waves had died down and gently lapped against the shore. Reed and Jess strolled along the dark wet sand with their shoes in their hands and the bottoms of their pants rolled up. Every few moments a wave would splash and send foam over their feet and up to their ankles.

"I smell something like paint," Jess said.

"Varnish," Reed said. "I gave *Simplicity* a coat tonight."

"*Simplicity*?"

"My sailboat," Reed said. "Well, it's my grandfather's, really. He left it to me when he died."

"Why do you have to varnish it?" Jess asked.

"She's a wooden boat so you've got to do it at least once a year to protect the wood."

"The whole boat?" Jess asked.

"Almost," Reed said. "I sand and paint the hull every spring while she's still in dry dock. Then I do the varnishing a bit at a time all summer while she's in the water."

"It must take a lot of time," Jess said.

"It's not bad. I usually work on her a couple of evenings a week and then on the weekends for a few hours."

"Do you ever have time to sail?" Jess asked, half joking.

Reed chuckled. "Sure, there's even time for that."

It was a battle for Jess to act calm and appear only mildly interested and friendly. Inside she was overflowing with questions she wanted to ask him, but she didn't want to appear nosy or too interested. Her insides felt as if they were at war with themselves. Part of her kept repeating what she already knew, that she had to be careful; he was a city guy and would never take her seriously. The other part of her just wanted to let go and be swept away by the rising tide of feelings she felt whenever he was close.

"What about you?" Reed asked.

"Me?" Jess was caught by surprise.

"What do you do when you're not being a lifeguard?"

"Oh, I don't know," Jess said. "The normal things. Read, watch TV, ride my bike, hang out with my friends."

"What about Andy?" Reed asked.

"He's a friend," Jess replied, almost too quickly.

Reed stopped and glanced at her. Almost automatically, they both turned and stared at the surf, just as if they were sharing the lifeguard chair during the day.

"I know that's what you told my brother," Reed said. "It's none of my business, but . . ." he started to add and then paused.

"Oh, it's okay, I don't mind," Jess said, turning to face him. She could feel her heart flutter. She felt as if she needed every ounce of reserve not to show the excitement of realizing that his interest in her went beyond work.

"Well, it's just that when I saw you on the beach tonight . . ." Reed said without finishing again.

"Oh, we were just goofing around," Jess said. "I mean, when you've been friends with someone as long as Andy and I have, it's . . . well, sometimes I think Andy might want it to be more, but we've just known each other too long. I strongly doubt anything could ever happen."

Jess bit her lip to stop herself from saying anything more. Could she possibly have been any more obvious?

Reed nodded and gazed away at the light surf. They were still standing beside each other, no more than a foot apart. Once again the memory of his arms around her flooded into Jess's mind. And again she knew it was his arms and not Andy's that she longed to feel. It was no use fighting the feeling. To pretend she wasn't attracted to him was to lie to herself. It didn't matter that he was from the city, or that they were both lifeguards sharing a lifeguard chair. The only thing that mattered was that she wanted to be with him.

Reed turned again and looked at her. The moonlight shimmered in her eyes and the light sea breeze lifted her beautiful blonde hair. He was fully aware of what he was feeling inside. . . .

"Reed?" someone shouted from up the beach.

Reed and Jess both turned. Paula was coming toward them.

When Reed told her he was going to work on that stupid sailboat of his that evening, Paula was disappointed, but not surprised. She'd come to accept the fact that he preferred varnishing to dancing. She could always find someone else to dance with, but it would be hard to find another boyfriend as handsome, rich, and well-liked as Reed. But when she'd called his house at nine-thirty and learned that he and Billy had gone out, *that* was cause for alarm.

Paula had gotten in her car and gone looking for them. She'd tried Rafe's ice-cream shop and had looked for their cars in the parking lot of the movie house. It had just been an accident that, after checking out the Crab Shack, she happened to see the fire on the beach and followed her hunch. A hunch that, as far as she was concerned, had just turned into a nightmare.

"Don't tell me," Paula said. "This is a seminar on night lifeguarding."

Jess quickly turned to Reed. "It was nice talking to you, Reed. I'll see you tomorrow."

Reed nodded and watched her walk away.

"Paula," he said. "I think it's time we had a talk."

NINE

The next day at the beach, Jess thought Reed was being quieter than usual. Hours passed while they carefully scanned the beach and the water without a word passing between them. Why wasn't he talking, she wondered? Was it because he was also afraid of what he was feeling? Was he worried he might say the wrong thing? She was dying to know what he was thinking. Had he felt what she'd felt the night before? Knowing what little she knew of him, and how serious he was about the job, did he think that it was impossible because they were lifeguards together? Oh, God! She hoped not! Did it frustrate him the way it did her?

Or maybe she was completely mistaken about him. After all, what had actually happened last night? They'd gone for a walk and talked, and then that witch Paula had interfered. There was nothing that Reed did or said that indicated anything more than that he was polite and friendly to her. Maybe it was just all wishful thinking on her part.

Wishful thinking? What was it that she wished would happen? That they'd fall madly in love for the balance of the summer and then not see each other for the next nine months while they went to their schools? No, *that was impossible!* She'd never survive, not if the feelings she'd already felt were any indication of what might follow. It made no sense. She had to stop herself before she got hurt. Besides, had she forgotten what he was? A guy from the city who went to a fancy prep school. Like Lisa said, some of them might be nicer than others, but you couldn't forget where they were from.

A mile away, Paula sat alone at a glass table, under an umbrella beside the pool at her parents' beach house. She sipped coffee sweetened with sugar and cream. Her hair hung like a limp mess, and this was one of those rare times when the light of day actually revealed her face with no makeup on it. Paula finished her coffee and hurled the cup into the tall hedge that surrounded the pool. She had never been so humiliated in her entire life. Who did Reed Petersen think he was? How dare he break up with her?

In an effort to be nice and so that she wouldn't be embarrassed, he had promised her he wouldn't tell anyone until she did. Paula knew that one of Reed's sore points was gossip. He just hated it. So of course Paula had immediately called several key friends who she knew would blab and announced that she'd broken off with Reed. She said he'd become moody and a drag, taking his silly lifeguarding so seriously and wanting to spend every free moment on his boring sailboat. But inside, Paula felt mortally stung. Reed had been her first serious relationship and she couldn't stand the idea that he'd been the one to end it.

After toying briefly with the idea of running away to Corfu to be with Spiro again, she hit upon a much more satisfying solution to her agony: revenge.

Sweet revenge . . . but what would it be? Paula hooked her limp black hair behind her ear as her brain began churning with ideas, but none of them was quite right. She could always start some particularly nasty rumors about Reed, but these days Reed seemed so cut off from the social scene, he might not even hear about them.

What else? *What else!?* As Paula pondered the possibilities, the skies overhead began to turn gray and darken. In the distance she could hear thunder. Oh, damn! she thought. On top of all the other terrible things that had happened, there was going to be a thunderstorm. Even her sunbathing would be ruined for the day.

Wait!

Paula straightened up in her chair. That was it, wasn't it? Of course! Suddenly Paula knew exactly what she was going to do.

It rained that afternoon and Hank told Lisa to go home. On the way, she stopped in town to window shop. It was just by accident, while in Attractions looking at clothes she could never afford to buy, that Lisa overheard two girls talking excitedly about Reed Petersen and Paula Lewis. Before she could get the whole story clearly, the girls went into the back where the dressing rooms were. Lisa quickly grabbed something off the rack and followed. The girls were in one dressing room. Lisa went into the one next door.

"I just can't believe she'd really break up with him," one of the girls said. "I mean, he's such a dreamboat."

"She said all he wants to do is be a lifeguard and sail," the other said. "She could never get him to go out dancing or do anything fun like that. She said she just couldn't stand it anymore."

"Who cares?" the first girl said. "Even if he were a monk, it would be worth it just to be able to go around saying that Reed Petersen was your boyfriend. I mean, not only is he gorgeous, but he's rich. So what if he wants to be a lifeguard?"

"Look, I'm only telling you what Paula told me," the other girl said. "If you ask me, I think she's crazy, too."

"Maybe she did it just to get him to pay more attention to her," the first girl said.

"Well, if she did, I hope she knows what she's doing," said the other. "Because once people hear they're not together anymore, I know a lot of girls who are going to be interested, myself included."

The girls started to talk about other things. Lisa was about to leave the dressing room when she happened to look at the dress she'd grabbed. It was yellow with black polka dots. Just out of curiosity, she checked the price tag. *$750!* Yikes! It would take her more than a month to earn that much. She hung it on a hook and left.

The next morning Lisa was driving to the beach when she saw Jess up ahead waiting at the bus stop for the beach bus. She immediately slowed down and rolled down the window.

"Want a ride?"

"Sure." Jess was glad Lisa had come along. The sky was gray and it looked as if it might rain at any moment. She pulled open the passenger door and slid into the seat next to her.

"Ready for another day with the patroons?" Lisa asked as she got back into traffic.

Jess smiled. Lisa had picked up "patroons" from Andy. It always sounded so funny when Lisa said it.

"If we get any today," Jess said. "Sure feels like another day of rain."

"With our luck there'll be big waves, and Gary Pilot and his friends will insist on boogie boarding in the rain all day," Lisa said. "So you want to hear some interesting gossip?"

"Okay."

"I was in Attractions yesterday looking at stuff I couldn't afford when I overheard two girls talking about Reed and his girlfriend, Paula," Lisa said. "So guess what? She broke up with him."

Jess quickly turned and stared at Lisa, then caught herself and gazed out the passenger window, trying not to look so interested. "Oh?"

"It seems that she's fed up with him just wanting to be a lifeguard and never wanting to party," Lisa said.

Jess couldn't help feeling disappointed. No wonder Reed had been so quiet the previous day. It wasn't what she'd imagined — that he was quiet because he was simply overwhelmed with emotions for her. It was all because Paula had broken up with him.

"The word is that every girl in Far Hampton will be after Reed as soon as the story gets around," Lisa said.

Jess smiled. "Including you?"

Lisa shook her head. "In my dreams. I'm too realistic to think I'd have much of a chance with a guy like that."

"You never know," Jess said, but she wondered if she was referring to Lisa or herself.

Billy had no idea why Paula had called and insisted on seeing him at the Crab Shack right away, and why it was so important that he not tell Reed. But it was his day off and kind of cloudy and dreary out. All he was doing was fooling around with his video stuff, so it was fine with him. His jeep was finally out of the shop, and he put the top up, got in, and drove to the Crab Shack.

The restaurant was practically empty, which

wasn't surprising considering it was ten-thirty on a cloudy Sunday morning. Billy went in and found Paula sitting at a table in the corner, wearing dark sunglasses and sipping a diet soda.

"What is this?" Billy asked. "An undercover operation?"

"Just sit," Paula said impatiently.

Billy sat down and lit a cigarette.

"Didn't anyone ever teach you manners?" Paula asked.

Billy frowned, then realized she meant his cigarette. "Oh, uh, sorry." He started to put it out.

"No, stupid," Paula snapped. "You're supposed to offer me one."

Billy glared at her. "Hey, look, I didn't come here so you could insult me." He started to get up.

"Don't go," Paula said irritably. "I'm sorry. I'm just in a really crappy mood. Now how about a cigarette?"

Billy gave her one and lit it. "I didn't know you smoked."

"I don't, except in times of major crisis," Paula replied.

"What's the crisis?"

"Reed didn't tell you?"

"No."

"Well, he broke up with me."

Billy pressed his lips together to keep from smiling. He'd never liked Paula. She was too stuck-up and snooty, even for his tastes.

"Why?" Billy asked.

"Because he's a jerk," Paula snapped. "Actually, there's another reason. I think it's his new lifeguarding partner, Jess Sloat."

Billy nodded. He'd suspected something was going on between those two. It was just like Reed to get the best-looking babe on the beach. Reed always got the best of everything, and Billy got the leftovers.

Paula tipped down her sunglasses. "How would you like Jess Sloat to be your girlfriend?"

Billy stared across the table at her. "I think you're a little psycho, Paula."

"I'm serious," Paula said.

"Why would Jess Sloat want to be my girlfriend?" Billy asked.

"Because I'd arrange it," Paula said.

"Like how?" Billy asked. "Just snap your fingers? Or do I have to give her Love Potion Number Nine?"

"No, all you have to do is get that Doppler radar out of the lifeguard shack and put it in the back of your brother's jeep," Paula said.

Billy just stared at her. "You're not just psycho, Paula, you're certifiable."

"Am I?" Paula asked. "Don't you ever get tired of being Reed Petersen's loser brother? Wouldn't you love the chance not only to get even with him, but to get Jess Sloat as well?"

It was a tempting thought, but Billy had strong doubts Paula could pull it off. "Even if I agreed to do it, how could I get into the lifeguard shack? Hank keeps it locked."

Paula smiled. "Don't you know about the spare key?"

Billy shook his head. No one had ever told him about a spare key to the lifeguard shack. Not that he'd ever had reason to be interested before.

"There's one spare key," Paula said as a smile formed on her lips. "Guess who has it?"

"Reed?"

"Bingo." Paula winked.

Billy shrugged. "So what if he does? It still doesn't make sense. Why would Reed want a Doppler radar?"

"For his sailboat," Paula said. "I've heard him say he'd love one, but they're too expensive. And you know how Reed hates to take money from your father."

Billy took a drag on his cigarette and blew a perfect smoke ring. He was impressed with how well Paula had thought out this little scam. The cops would find the radar in the back of Reed's jeep. They'd know he had the only spare key. Now that Billy thought about it, even he could recall Reed saying how great it would be to have that kind of radar on his sailboat.

"I gotta hand it to you," Billy said. "You really figured this one out beautifully."

Paula couldn't help smiling. "I know. So you'll do it?"

Billy crushed out his cigarette and stood. "No, thanks. I may hate my brother, but I don't hate him enough to get him in that much trouble."

Paula clenched her teeth and watched Billy walk out of the Crab Shack. Just wait, Billy boy, she thought. Just wait.

Rainy days were usually gifts to the lifeguards because Hank would send half of them home and keep a skeleton crew in the chairs. But today Jess prayed it wouldn't rain. She wanted to sit with Reed and see how he acted. The lifeguards were gathered outside the shack when she and Lisa got there. Reed had been talking to Ellie, but when he saw Jess, he came toward her with a bounce in his step.

"Hey, what's up?" He seemed excited to see her. Yesterday Hank had sent her home because of the rain, so they hadn't seen each other. Once again, Jess felt that tingling, magnetic sensation. She'd never felt anything like it before. She only wanted to be with him. If he'd asked her to join him on a trek through a mosquito-infested swamp, she was sure she would have said yes.

"I don't know," she said, feeling a smile on her face. "What's up with you?"

"Well, I, uh, missed you yesterday," Reed said.

"You did?" Jess didn't know whether she was more surprised or happy.

"Well, sure," Reed said. "You think it's fun sitting alone in the rain all day?"

"You can always talk to the sea gulls," Jess said.

"Nah." Reed shook his head. "All they ever want to talk about is fish and the weather."

Jess grinned.

"And talk about *this* weather," Reed said. "Looks like we might get rain again today. Hank's been tracking the storm on the Doppler radar all morning. You should see him. He's like a kid with a new toy."

"I guess, in a way, he is," Jess said.

Reed chuckled. "Some toy."

"Where is he, anyway?" Jess asked.

"Inside the shack," Reed said. "He'll be out in a second."

Reed seemed cheerful this morning. Jess was dying to ask him about Paula. Could she just come right out and ask? It seemed too bold. On the other hand, she hated hinting around at things and playing games.

"I heard a rumor," she said.

Reed looked at her curiously. "What?"

"That Paula broke up with you."

Reed's expression instantly changed. His smile disappeared and he suddenly seemed guarded. "You heard *she broke up with me?*"

"Like I said. It was just a rumor," Jess said. "I mean, I don't even know if it's true."

Reed just nodded, but said nothing. Now Jess regretted bringing it up. He obviously wasn't happy about it. She wished she'd kept her mouth shut.

A drop of rain hit her on the head. Then another and another. A lifeguard named Stu knocked on the door of the lifeguard shack. "Hey, Hank," he called. "Give us a word."

The door opened and Hank stuck his head out and looked up at the sky. Then he turned to the crew. "The radar shows a whole line of storms coming through with this cold front. Today's going to be a washout. All senior guards man your chairs. The rest of you can scoot."

Without a word, Reed turned and headed for

the Main chair. Jess couldn't let him go like that. Impulsively, she reached out and grabbed his arm. "Reed?"

He turned and gazed steadily at her without answering.

"I didn't mean to upset you," Jess said.

"I know you didn't," Reed replied.

"Well, I guess I just don't understand," Jess said. "You seemed like you were in a good mood. Then I told you about the rumor and now you seem really bummed."

The rain was starting to come down harder. Reed looked up at the sky and then back to Jess. "It's a long story, Jess."

"That's okay," Jess said. It wasn't as if she had a lot to do that day now that Hank was sending her home.

But Reed shook his head. "I've got to get in the chair. I'll see you tomorrow."

He turned and walked away. Jess watched, uncertain whether he was angry with her or not.

TEN

The fact that Reed insisted on keeping his breakup with Paula a secret had certain advantages. As a once-frequent visitor to Breezes, Paula knew Helene, the housekeeper, fairly well. So when she showed up at the mansion the next day saying Reed had asked her to stop by and pick up something for him, Helene was more than willing to let her into his room. Paula knew she had plenty of time. Both Reed and Billy were working at the beach, and Mr. Petersen was away on a business trip as usual. Paula settled herself at Reed's desk. Reed did all of his writing on a Macintosh computer. Paula turned it on and quickly drafted a letter that would suit her purposes.

CONFIDENTIAL

Dear Hank,

I regret having to write you this letter concerning Billy, but for the sake of lifeguard morale and the safety of the patrons, I think there are some things you should know.

Billy smokes in the chair when he thinks he can get away with it. He frequently drinks beer in public when he's not on duty. While in the chair he often listens to music and spends a good deal of time trying to impress girls by ordering Andy around.

I know that it's your policy to give people a chance to prove themselves and you obviously thought Billy deserved a shot at being a senior guard. However, I'm afraid that Billy isn't up to the job. As long as Billy is a senior guard, I'm convinced we run a risk that might prove fatal in a crisis situation.

Sincerely,

Reed

A few moments later she printed two copies of the letter. Forging Reed's name was no problem. The night before, Paula had taken out a few of his old letters and practiced copying his signature until she had it down perfectly. Paula signed both letters and studied them. She smiled. It looked quite authentic. She stood up and almost turned off the computer.

Wait, there was one last thing she had to do. She saved the letter in a file marked *Billy*.

Three days later Billy came out of the lifeguard shack reeling. Hank had just demoted him back to regular lifeguard. The lifeguard captain practically had a laundry list of offenses Billy had committed in the chair — from smoking to using Andy Moncure to show off to girls. But the thing that really killed Billy were the offenses Hank knew about that Billy had committed off duty. There was only one way that Hank could have known that Billy drank beer on the beach at night — someone had ratted on him.

Who knew about all these things? There was only one person — Andy Moncure. He had to be the one who told. It made perfect sense. Billy knew that Andy had hoped he'd be made a senior guard that year instead of Billy. So when Billy got the promotion instead, Andy just waited until the time was right and then nailed him. Billy's hands curled into fists. Andy must have been gloating, thinking he'd really put one over on Billy. But Billy would have the last laugh. He was going to go back to the chair and turn that kid into hamburger helper. He was so mad he didn't even care if it meant getting canned as a lifeguard for good.

Halfway between the lifeguard shack and the East Wing chair, Paula was waiting for Billy. Billy was so blind with rage he almost didn't see her as he stormed through the sand thinking about how he was going to tear Andy limb from limb.

"Billy?"

"Huh?" Billy looked up. It took a second for him to focus. "What, Paula?"

"What's wrong?" Paula asked. "You look like you want to kill someone."

"Yeah? Well, that's because I do," Billy said.

"What happened?"

"That geek Andy ratted on me to Hank. He got me demoted back to regular lifeguard as of tomorrow."

"How do you know it was him?" Paula asked.

Something about her tone of voice caused a warning bell to go off in Billy's head. He squinted at her. "What do you know about this, Paula?"

"Nothing," Paula said with well-practiced innocence. "Why would I know anything?"

"It was just the way you asked," Billy said. "I mean, it had to be Andy who told. He's the only one who knew I smoked in the chair and drank beer on the beach at night."

Paula laughed. "Are you serious, Billy? Everyone knows you do those things."

Maybe she was right. Billy stared at her. "What's your point, Paula?"

"My point is, what good is it going to do if you beat up Andy?" Paula asked. "You'll only get yourself fired and make Andy look like a hero."

"Maybe, but he'll look like a real black-and-blue hero," Billy said.

"And in a week the black-and-blue marks will be gone and you'll still be out of a lifeguarding job," Paula reminded him. "You're too smart to do something that dumb."

"So what do you suggest I do?" Billy asked.

"Why don't you talk to Andy first," Paula said. "Mention a few things and see if he acts guilty. You're smart enough to tell whether he's putting on an act."

But Billy was still suspicious. "Why are you telling me this, Paula? I mean, don't tell me it's out of the goodness of your heart."

"Maybe it's because I'm hoping that if I help you with this, you'll change your mind and help me with Reed," Paula said.

"No way." Billy shook his head. "I told you there's no way I'm going to get my brother in that much trouble."

"Okay, then maybe I'll come up with something else for Reed," Paula said. "In the meantime, talk to Andy and then meet me at the Crab Shack after work."

Sitting next to Reed in the Main chair, Jess felt uncomfortable. Because of rain and her day off, several days had gone by since she'd last seen him. She wished he'd called her at home, but he hadn't, and as the days passed she convinced herself that he really didn't like her. Reed was usually quiet when they sat in the chair, and today was no exception. Jess couldn't tell if he was mad at her or not. All morning he'd been quiet and polite. She kept waiting, no . . . *hoping* that he'd give her some kind of sign. Anything was better than leaving her wondering. But now Jess felt too cautious to ask.

The phone in the chair rang and Reed answered it and spoke briefly before hanging up.

"Hank wants me," he said, getting up and starting down the ladder. "Be right back."

Jess always felt a mild sense of nervousness when Reed left the chair. After all, he was leaving her alone to watch over the busiest, most crowded part of the beach. Today she was especially nervous. It was the moon tide, that one day a month when the moon was full and the tides were exaggerated. The waves were higher than usual and breaking close to shore, and the undertow and rip currents were strong. Fortunately it was the kind of day when few people had the nerve to venture past the breaking waves. Still, she had to keep an eye out.

It was difficult for Billy to control his impulses. Sitting there in the chair with Andy, he just wanted to smash the kid in the face. The amazing thing was that Andy acted as if he didn't even know what was going on.

"So what did Hank want you for?" he asked when Billy got back to the chair.

"Like you don't know?" Billy shot back.

Andy frowned and shook his head. "How would I know?"

Good acting, jerko, Billy thought. "I just got busted down from senior guard. Starting tomorrow I'm back to regular lifeguard."

"You serious?" Andy looked honestly surprised.

"Give me a break, Moncure," Billy said sourly.

"What do you mean, give you a break?" Andy said. "A break about what?"

Either the kid was telling the truth or he was a great actor, Billy thought. But if he was telling the truth, then who had ratted on him?

"Maybe you can tell me something," Billy said. "Maybe you can tell me how Hank knew I sneak butts in the chair and drink on the beach at night when he's nowhere around?"

He watched the expression on Andy's face change from puzzlement to fear.

"Hey, I know what you're thinking," Andy said. "Forget it. I'm not the one who ratted. No way. You think I'd do that and then come back here and sit with you? I might as well blindfold myself and lie down on the train tracks. I'm serious, man, I don't know who told Hank about that stuff, but you'd better believe it wasn't me."

Billy stared at him. As much as he hated to admit it, it sounded like Andy was telling the truth. But if Andy hadn't ratted on him, then who had?

A group of half a dozen younger girls caught Jess's eye. They'd congregated right at the edge of the surf and were playing in the runoff after each large wave crashed. Soon the playing evolved into a game of dare as the girls tried to see how far into the water they could get and still race out before the next big wave crashed.

It was a game people of all ages played nearly every day. Usually there was nothing wrong with it. The worst that might happen was that you got caught by a wave and rolled up the beach with the white bubbling foam. But today wasn't the usual kind of day.

It was up to the lifeguard to decide whether the game was harmless or dangerous. If it was dangerous, she could whistle them to stop.

The girls laughed and squealed happily as they dashed up the beach just ahead of the next wave. Jess brought her whistle to her lips, but seeing how much fun they were having, she hesitated.

A moment later it was too late.

The undertow from the runoff was too strong. Several of the girls were able to run through it, but one stumbled and fell to her knees. Jess had caught a glimpse of the look of horror on the girl's face as she looked back over her shoulder and saw a huge wave rise up and then engulf her like a hungry predator.

Jess launched herself off the lifeguard stand, hit the sand, and grabbed a torp. A moment later she was racing toward the spot where the girl had disappeared under the wave. Already her friends were rushing to the edge of the water, pointing and shouting. Just before she entered the water, Jess heard one girl shout the name Cheryl Marie.

By the time Jess was waist deep in the water, she could feel the undertow like a torrent dragging her farther out. Another huge wave rose up and Jess dove under it and kept swimming, trying to get past the surf and figure out where the current would take the young girl.

Moments later she surfaced just beyond the breaking surf. A new set of waves was rolling in, lifting and dropping her just before curling and crashing onto the beach. The currents swirled violently and Jess knew this was a particularly dangerous place to be. Should she be swept just a few feet closer to shore she could be caught in a curling wave and slammed down into the sand.

Suddenly a head popped out of the water just a few feet from her. It was the girl! Her face half covered with wet brown hair like a sheep dog, she began gasping for breath and thrashing desperately.

"Cheryl Marie!" Jess shouted.

For a moment, the girl stopped thrashing and

looked stunned that someone so close had called her name.

"Cheryl Marie!" Jess shouted again, knowing that calling her name would reassure the girl. She kicked hard through the water, pushing the torp ahead of her. "You're going to be okay. Just grab this."

The girl reached out desperately and grabbed the rope that ran around the torp.

"You're going to be okay!" Jess shouted as she treaded water in the turbulent current. "Just hold on and I'll bring you back in through the surf, okay, Cheryl Marie?"

The girl nodded, her face still partly covered with wet hair. "But I'm Marie," she gasped. "Not . . ."

"Help!" a voice shouted.

Jess spun around in the water. There was another girl thrashing in the water ten feet away!

"Cheryl!" Marie cried.

There were two of them! Not Cheryl Marie . . . Cheryl and Marie! Now what was she going to do? A torp was really only good for one victim. . . . There was no way she could get both girls through this surf and back to the beach at the same time!

"Help!" Cheryl cried in a watery, garbled voice and then disappeared under the surface.

With a rush of adrenaline, Jess swam toward her and dove, feeling desperately through the sand-clouded swirling water. She got a handful of hair and pulled up. It wasn't the most glamorous rescue, but it was the fastest. Kicking toward the surface, she managed to get Cheryl's head out of the water. The girl coughed and sputtered, but at least she was breathing.

Another huge swell swept past them, bringing them practically into the surf. Jess quickly slid her arm around the coughing girl's chest and swam toward Marie who was still clinging to the torp.

"What should I do?" Marie cried.

"Just hold on!" Jess shouted. "Hold on!"

She grabbed the end of the buoy with her free hand. Then, with one arm around Cheryl and one hand on the torp, she tried to kick back out, fighting to keep the girls away from the breaking waves. But swell after swell swept them back toward the surf. It was impossible. Without the use of her arms, Jess couldn't get anywhere, but she couldn't let go of Marie or Cheryl, either. Gasping and coughing herself as she swallowed water, she kicked as hard as she could while struggling to keep the girls on the surface. Her legs felt as if they were going to cramp. Each time a new swell lifted them, she was certain this was the one that would curl into a wave and dash them down into the sand.

Just when Jess thought she couldn't take another kick, she felt Cheryl suddenly yank away. Jess looked around and came face to face with Ellie!

"I've got this one, Jess!" Ellie shouted.

Next she saw Stu swimming toward her. "You're tired," he shouted at Jess as he reached for Marie. "I'll take this one in. Look out for the surf."

Another swell lifted them. Ellie and Stu were starting to swim in with the two girls, leaving Jess to go in on her own. She took a deep breath and followed. With two sharp kicks of her legs, she propelled herself into the curling, crashing waves. A split second later she tumbled in the turbulent water like socks in a clothes washer.

Jess hit the sand with her shoulder and felt it scrape hard against her skin. She knew she was underwater but had no idea how deep she was. It was impossible to swim to the surface because she was being twirled around so much she couldn't tell which way was up. She was so tired from the rescue that all she could do was hold her breath and wait until the wave let go.

It was probably only a few seconds, but it seemed like an eternity. Suddenly a pair of strong hands slid under her armpits and pulled her up. Jess felt herself rise up out of the water. She felt the air and opened her mouth to gasp for breath. Fresh air had never tasted so good! She felt an arm go across her chest. Thank God someone had come in and grabbed her. She opened her eyes.

It was Reed.

"You okay?" he asked, his arm still tight around her chest.

"I think so."

He started to pull her out of the water. A few seconds later they reached the beach. Once Reed could stand, he slid his arms under her and carried her up like a groom carrying his bride across the threshold. Jess shivered. The sudden exertion had left her exhausted. Feeling drained and weak, she pressed her cheek against his hard warm chest and allowed his strong arms to enfold her. For that moment she forgot about the rescue, about how close she'd come to drowning, about the crashing of the waves and the crowded noisy beach around them. She only wished she could just stay in his arms forever, feeling warm and protected.

ELEVEN

"Look, Jess, I won't fault you on bravery," Hank said. They were sitting in the lifeguard shack, alone. Jess still had a dry towel wrapped around her shoulders, even though she had warmed up and didn't really need it anymore. The rescue had been a success. Both Marie and Cheryl made it back to shore having suffered no more than a few scratches, a couple of mouthfuls of salt water, and a good scare.

Hank waited until everyone had calmed down and the beach had gotten back to normal. Then he called Jess and asked her to come to the shack.

"Do you know what you did wrong?" Hank asked.

Jess shook her head.

"You didn't take time to assess the situation," the lifeguard captain said. "I know your immediate reaction was to act fast before one of those girls drowned, but you should have taken just a moment more. Then you would have seen that there were two swimmers in distress and handled the situation accordingly."

Jess nodded. She knew he was right.

Hank came over and put his hand on the top of her head. She could feel the sand lodged in her wet hair as he rubbed her head fondly. "You did good, Jess. You succeeded at a difficult rescue and learned a lesson. Now get back out there."

Jess left the lifeguard shack, walked back out into the bright sun, and over to the Main chair.

She looked up and saw that Reed was looking back over the Main chair at her.

"Shouldn't you be watching the patroons?" Jess asked.

"I just wanted to make sure you were okay," Reed said. Then he did something he'd never done before. He reached down and gave her a hand as she climbed up into the chair.

"Thanks, but I really don't need the special treatment," Jess said once she got into the chair. "All I managed to do was get rolled by a wave."

"I thought you did a little more than that," Reed said. "You saved two lives. What did Hank say?"

"That I was brave, but I should have assessed the situation better."

Reed smiled. "Well, what do you expect?"

Jess gave him a puzzled look. "I don't follow."

"I guess he felt like he had to say something," Reed said. "But the truth is, you did the best you could in an unpredictable situation. Sometimes things just happen. You can't plan or prepare for them. You just have to react the best way you know."

Sometimes things just happen . . .

She knew he was referring to the rescue, but it was strange how the words applied to so many other things. Oddly, Jess felt relieved. At least he was being friendly and talking to her again.

Reed leaned toward her and held her with his dark eyes. The memory of his arms cradling her was still fresh in her thoughts. "I think Hank's right. You were incredibly brave. A lot of lifeguards would have looked at the size of that surf and immediately called for help." He smiled, then reached out and placed his hand on her arm, squeezing it. "You've got a lot of guts, Jess."

Jess felt slightly dizzy. She knew it was partly the after-affect of exerting herself so hard. But it was also his words, and the sincere, affectionate tone of his voice.

Sometimes things just happen . . .

Now that Paula had broken up with him, would something just happen between them? No, that *was* something she could have control over. And her mind said no, a thousand times, no.

Paula had been too busy plotting to catch all of the excitement that afternoon, but she had gotten down to the water in time to see Reed carry Jess out of the surf and then watch that conniving little blonde lifeguard melt into Reed's arms. It was enough to make her sick, and more than enough to make her yearning for revenge even stronger. How dare that little wench try to steal Reed Petersen from her? Who did she think she was dealing with?

Paula planned to take care of both Reed and Jess, but right now she had to make sure she led Billy away from Andy and toward his brother. Actually, thanks to the sudden excitement, it wouldn't be as hard as she thought.

It was almost dinnertime and the Crab Shack was crowded. Billy finally found Paula sitting at one of the picnic tables outside, wearing her sunglasses again. He slumped down opposite her and lit a cigarette.

"Want one?"

Paula shook her head. "Did you talk to Andy?"

"Yeah."

"And?"

"It's hard to tell," Billy said. "But if I had to bet, I'd bet he wasn't the one who ratted."

"You're right." Paula smiled.

Billy squinted at her suspiciously. "How would you know?"

Paula opened her bag and took out a badly wrinkled letter. She smoothed it on the picnic table and then slid it toward Billy. It was actually the second of the two copies she'd printed out on Reed's computer, but there was no way Billy could know that.

"What's this?" Billy asked, taking the letter.

"Have a look."

She watched Billy's expression change as he read through the letter. By the time he finished, his eyes were practically bulging out of his head. He looked up at Paula with his mouth agape.

"No," he said, shaking his head. "I don't believe it."

"You said that Reed always had to be better than you," Paula said. "It looks to me like he just couldn't stand the idea that you were a senior guard, too, and therefore his equal."

Billy squinted at her and held up the letter. "If this letter is real, how'd you get it?"

"You remember the little excitement we had this afternoon? When Jess went out to make that rescue? Hank came out on the beach. Everyone was so busy watching that I just slipped into the lifeguard shack and looked around. I found this in the garbage can."

Billy stared down at the letter again as if he couldn't make up his mind whether he believed her or not.

"Look, Billy," Paula said. "If you don't want to believe me, I don't really care. I just think it's a shame that you'd let Reed do something like this to you and not want to get back at him."

Billy narrowed his eyes. "I still don't see what you get out of this, Paula. Why do you want my brother to get into trouble?"

Paula leaned forward and tipped her glasses down. "He dropped me, Billy. No boy has ever dropped me before. As far as I'm concerned, there's no trouble I could get him into that would be enough."

It had been a long afternoon for Andy. Like almost everyone else on the beach, he'd come running as soon as he'd seen the crowd forming in front of the Main chair. He'd seen Jess struggling out in the waves with the two girls and had seen Ellie and Stu go out and bring them in.

And then, like everyone else on the beach, he'd seen how Jess collapsed into Reed's arms and how he'd carried her up the beach. Maybe to most other people it appeared to be an innocent act. Just one exhausted lifeguard needing her partner's support. But to Andy it had a special meaning. It meant that he'd had his chance and he hadn't taken it. Now Reed Petersen, a slick guy from the city, would make sure he never got a second chance.

Why, Jess? Andy wanted to ask her. Why, of all the guys in the world, did you have to pick *him?*

At the end of the day, Andy climbed down from the chair and trudged back through the sand toward the parking lot. He was just passing the lifeguard shack when Hank called through the open door to him.

"Andy?"

Andy felt a chill run up his spine. He'd been dreading this moment all day. "Yeah, Hank?"

"Come in for a second, will you?"

Andy stepped slowly into the shack. After what had happened to Billy that afternoon, he had a feeling he was going to be in big trouble. He probably should have told Hank about Billy a long time ago. By keeping it a secret he was almost like Billy's accomplice, as if he had contributed as much to a situation that was dangerous for patroons as Billy had.

"Have a seat, Andy," Hank said. Lisa was sitting on the edge of the computer table. Andy wasn't sure why she was there, but he said hello.

"Hi, Andy," Lisa replied.

Andy took a deep breath. Unlike Billy, he couldn't be demoted. All he was was a regular lifeguard. The only thing Hank could do was fire him. Andy slumped down in the chair and stared at the sand-covered floor. Boy, what a day. First it looked like he'd lost Jess, now it looked like he was going to lose his job. A spark of anger lit a small fire in him. Why hadn't Billy gotten canned? The answer was obvious. Billy came from a rich, powerful family. The Petersens had too much influence in town. Billy was like some diplomat's kid, immune from the law. The worst punishment Hank could give him was to slap his hand.

"I'm disappointed in you, Andy," Hank began. "You knew what Billy was up to and you didn't say anything."

Andy kept staring down at the floor. This is it, he thought. He could feel the ax start to fall.

"I know you're aware that by allowing Billy to fool around like that, you were putting the lives of other people into jeopardy," the lifeguard captain said.

Andy nodded. He was already wondering

what he would do for the rest of the summer. Mow lawns? The thought just killed him. He loved being a lifeguard, sitting in that chair every day. Looking forward to it was the only thing that got him through the long boring winters out here.

"However," Hank said, "I'm also aware of how hard it would be for a person in your position to rat on your senior guard. Especially when that senior guard is Billy Petersen."

Andy nodded again. He didn't know why Hank was drawing it out so long. He should have just canned him and been done with it.

"I assume that you're aware that Billy has been demoted back to the rank of regular lifeguard," Hank said.

Andy nodded again.

"The question then becomes, who will take Billy's place as senior guard in the East Wing chair?" Hank said.

Why ask me? Andy thought.

"Think you're up to the job?" Hank asked.

Andy looked up, puzzled. Who was Hank asking? Had someone else come into the shack? All he saw was Hank and Lisa. It couldn't be Lisa. She was just a rookie.

"Me?" Andy asked incredulously.

Hank nodded. "I assume you've learned

an important lesson and won't let it happen
again."

"Huh? Oh, uh, yeah, sure," Andy stammered,
still stunned by the sudden turn of events.

"Good," Hank said with a smile. "Starting
tomorrow, you'll be the senior guard in the East
Wing chair. Billy will be reassigned to sit with
Ellie in the West Wing. Lisa here will be your
partner. I asked her to stay so that you two could
have a little time to talk and prepare to work
together."

The next thing Andy knew, Hank was shaking
his hand. They all left the lifeguard shack and
Hank locked the door behind them.

"Okay, see you two bright and early," the
lifeguard captain said and headed for the parking
lot. Andy stood on the porch of the lifeguard
shack, still feeling completely shocked.

"You look surprised," Lisa said.

"I am," Andy admitted. "I thought for sure
he was gonna fire me."

"Why?"

"For not telling him about all the stuff Billy
was doing," Andy said.

"I think Hank understands why you didn't
tell," Lisa said. "Anyway, I think it'll be fun for
us to work together."

Andy turned and stared back down the beach

at the East Wing chair. Now that the patroons
had departed, the sea gulls had landed on the
sand for their daily afternoon scavenger hunt,
picking up every morsel of food and snack left
behind. He still couldn't believe it. Hank had
made him a senior guard! Incredible.

"Aren't you happy?" Lisa asked.

Andy sat down on the edge of the lifeguard
shack porch and stared out at the waves. "I don't
know, I guess."

Lisa sat down next to him. Andy thought she
was a cute girl, with her short black hair and
turned-up nose and pixielike smile. As a person,
Andy liked her. But as a rookie lifeguard, he
wondered if she was big enough and strong
enough to make a rescue. Now he was going to
have to depend on her.

Lisa pulled her knees up to her chest and stared
at the crashing waves. The air had turned cool
and an incoming breeze brought the scent of the
sea. An hour ago, when Hank had first informed
her that she'd be sharing the East Wing chair
with Andy, she'd been incredibly happy. Now
she was worried. Andy didn't seem very excited
for someone who'd just been made a senior
guard. Was it because he'd just learned that she
was to be his partner?

"Andy?" Lisa said.

"Oh, uh, yeah?" He turned and gave her a quizzical look.

"Are you all right?"

"Yeah, just a little surprised, that's all." Andy stared back at the ocean again. His insides were a jumble of feelings.

Lisa was still worried. Being a firm believer in getting things out in the open, she gathered up her courage. "You're not upset that I'm going to be your partner, are you?"

"No, no, it's nothing like that," Andy said.

"Then what is it?" Lisa asked.

Next to her Andy sighed. "You really want to know?"

"Sure."

"It's Jess. I think she's falling for Reed Petersen."

Lisa knew that Jess and Reed had been together a lot lately, but it seemed more than natural for two people who were sharing a lifeguard chair. Even that afternoon, when Reed had carried Jess in his arms, Lisa had just assumed he was being supportive.

"How do you know?" Lisa asked.

Andy shrugged. "I just do. It's what I see when they're together, it's the way Jess has been acting. I've known Jess for a long time."

"Has she ever really liked someone before?" Lisa asked.

"Oh, sure, plenty of them," Andy said. "But I always got the feeling . . . or maybe it was that she always gave me the impression that they weren't serious."

"You think it's different with Reed?" Lisa asked.

"Yeah, I do. I can't explain why. Maybe it's something about him. I just get the feeling that if Jess is going to be involved with him, it's going to be serious."

"Well, maybe it's the right time for her," Lisa said.

Andy nodded slowly. "Yeah, maybe it is."

At first Lisa didn't understand why Andy seemed so disturbed. Jess had told her that she and Andy were just very good friends. But it was starting to be obvious that Andy felt differently. Lisa almost wanted to kick herself for not having figured it out sooner. Then again, maybe it was something she hadn't wanted to figure out.

"Andy?" she said softly. "Is the reason why you're upset because you have more than just friendly feelings toward Jess?"

Andy nodded slowly and Lisa felt her heart sink. So that was it. She should have guessed.

Lisa pulled her knees in closer and rested her chin on them. The sun was starting to turn pink in the western sky. Once again she had the dubious distinction of picking the wrong guy.

Next to her, Andy reached down and picked up a handful of sand. Together they watched as he let the grains slip down through his fingers.

"You know what's weird?" Andy asked. "Jess and I have been friends for all these years. And she's always been beautiful. I mean, by sixth grade I knew my best friend was the most wanted girl in the class. But she was always just a friend to me. I just never thought of her as anything else. Then one day, just a couple of weeks ago, it all changed. I still can't figure out why."

"Know what I think?" Lisa said. "I think feelings are things that don't make sense. You'll never be able to figure out why. Something just changes one day. There may be a reason, but it's not one you'll ever know."

Andy turned and stared at her. "So what do you think I should do now?"

The question caught Lisa totally off guard. What should Andy do about Jess? *Forget about her!* she wanted to shout. Look at who's sitting right next to you. A perfectly cute, nice girl who likes you. But of course she couldn't say that. Andy was obviously in no condition to hear it.

"I think you have to wait and see," Lisa heard herself reply. "If it's going to be serious between Jess and Reed, there's probably nothing you can do about it. If it's not serious, that's a whole different story."

Inside, Lisa was starting to hope that whatever developed between Reed and Jess would be *very* serious.

"You don't think it would do any good to talk to her?" Andy asked.

"I guess you could," Lisa said. "I'm just not sure what you'd say. I mean, from what you've told me, even Jess doesn't know whether it's going to be serious or not with Reed."

"Yeah, you're right." Andy leaned his elbows on his knees and stared down at the sand. Lisa resisted the temptation to slide her arm across his shoulders and hug him. He looked so sad and lonely. She just wanted to shake him and say, *Jess isn't the only girl in the world. There are others. Just look around.*

But like everything else she wished she could say, this was something that would never leave her lips.

TWELVE

That evening, on the second floor of his home, Billy slipped out of his room and quietly walked down the hall. Reed was down at the dock working on his stupid sailboat as usual. Billy slipped into his brother's room and closed the door behind him. The moon was full and the moonlight sent shadows into the room. Without turning on a light, Billy sat down at Reed's desk. If his brother had written the letter, he would have done it on his computer. Billy flicked on the Mac. A dozen files flashed onto the screen. Some were computer games, some were programs. One was labeled Documents. Billy called the file up. In it were two dozen letters, some to Paula, some to various aunts and uncles. Then Billy saw the one labeled with his own name.

He clicked the mouse. In a flash the letter appeared on the screen. By the time Billy finished reading, it took all of his willpower not to heave the computer right out the window. So Paula was right. It was Reed who'd ratted. The brat just couldn't stand the idea of his brother being as good as he was. Well, if Reed wanted to fight dirty, he was going to have to start taking lessons from the master.

It didn't take Billy long to find the spare key to the lifeguard shack. It was lying in Reed's top drawer with a piece of orange cord tied to it in a clove hitch or one of those other stupid knots they were all supposed to learn. Billy slid the key into his pocket and left the room. It looked like he'd be making another trip to the beach tonight.

Jess sat alone on the screened-in porch, staring out at the full moon. The air was clear tonight and she could see the moon so distinctly that it was almost startling. She was glad she was sitting on the porch. It was the quietest place in the house, although the truth was there was no really quiet place. She shared a small ranch house with her family and almost every night her nine-year-old brother, Tommy, played Nintendo, her father watched a baseball game, and her mother listened to oldies music from the fifties and sixties while she sewed.

So Jess chose to sit on a padded outdoor chair on the small porch where the loudest noises were the screeching of the cicadas, the sounds of traffic drifting over from the highway, and the voices of her neighbors fighting.

She was thinking about Reed. It was hardly surprising. He was all she thought about anymore. The constant war between her head and her heart actually tired her. Her head continually screaming *NO!* as loudly as her heart shouted *YES!* And after all the excitement of the rescue today, she was almost exhausted.

"Jess?" It was her father.

Jess quickly sat up straighter. She could see her father's outline in the doorway. He was six feet tall with sandy-colored hair that was starting to look very thin on top, broad shoulders, and each year a little more paunch around the belt line than the year before. He was wearing the navy-blue pants and short-sleeved shirt that were the summer uniform of the Far Hampton police force.

"Yes, Dad?"

"I couldn't find you inside."

"I came out here. It was a little noisy."

"You call this quiet?" her father asked with a smile. The chorus of crickets and cicadas was almost deafening.

Jess smiled back. "No, but I guess it's just a different kind of noise.'

Her father gestured to a chair. "Mind if I join you?"

Jess shook her head. Even if she had, she wouldn't have said so. Her father sat down and gazed out at the sky.

"That's some moon tonight, huh?" he said.

"I've been looking at it."

"I always meant to buy you a telescope," her father said. "You've always loved looking at the moon and stars. I just never quite got together enough money to get a good one."

"It's okay, Dad," Jess said. "I'm happy looking at them with my eyes. Besides, if I ever wanted to use a telescope, there's one over at school."

"I know," he said. "But it would have been nice if you could have had one at home. It's just that between paying all the bills and saving for you and Tommy to go to college — "

"Dad," Jess interrupted him. "I don't feel deprived."

Her father ran his fingers through his thinning hair. "I never know whether you're telling me the truth or just trying to make sure I don't feel bad."

"In general it's about fifty/fifty," Jess replied with a smile.

Her father smiled back. "So I hear you had some excitement over at the beach this afternoon."

"How'd you hear?" Jess asked, surprised.

"It's a small town, Jess. Word gets around. I heard you were very brave but, if you'll excuse the expression, in over your head."

"I know," Jess said. "I went out to rescue one person and it turned out there were two. I couldn't handle both with the equipment I had."

"But I also heard that you hung tough and didn't panic, Jess," her father said. "You can learn not to make the same mistake next time. But guts and common sense are things you have to be born with. I'm proud of you."

For a second he reminded her of what Reed had said. Jess smiled in the dark. "Thanks, Dad."

He looked down at his watch. "The Mets have a late start on the West Coast tonight. I guess I'll try to catch the first few innings before I fall asleep." He started to get up.

"Dad?" Jess said. "Can I ask you a question?"

Her father stopped and looked back at her in the dark. "Sure."

"What do you know about the Petersens?"

Even in the dark, she could see her father frown. "The company or the family?"

"Both."

"Well, I know that about twenty years ago Charlie Petersen started buying up farmland and beachfront property around here and built luxury homes that only people from the city could afford. Most of them sold as summer places. Of course, he became enormously wealthy in the process. I can't fault him for that, but what happened was, once all the merchants around here found out what people paid in the city, they all upped their prices. Now that might not have made any difference to the people from the city, but it sure made life harder for those of us who work out here. You remember what an ice-cream cone used to cost at Rafe's?"

"Sure," Jess said. "I used to get two scoops of any flavor for fifty cents."

"Now that cone would cost you two-fifty," her father said. "And the same thing happened with clothes and furniture and groceries and all the things we need to get along. There was a time when the police chief earned one of the highest salaries in town, next to the mayor. Now I don't even make as much as my plumber."

"But is that really Mr. Petersen's fault?" Jess asked.

"No, not entirely," her father admitted. "I'm sure he didn't have anything like that in mind when he started out. He just wanted to build homes and sell them. But frankly, I think we would have been a lot better off if Charlie Petersen had picked some other town to develop and left us alone."

"You've talked mostly about the company," Jess said. "What about the family?"

"Well, Gail Petersen died about five years ago. She was a good lady. Gave a lot of money to charity and even made her husband build some middle-income housing so that teachers and town workers could afford to live in the town they worked in. There used to be a joke that Gail gave it away almost as fast as Charlie made it. Of course, that wasn't even close to the truth, but it did help make us locals feel a little more friendly to her husband's company than if they'd just come in and squeezed out every dollar they could."

"And what happened after she died?"

"Well, Charlie's a businessman. Making money is what he knows how to do. He doesn't have his wife's charitable spirit."

"And the rest of the family?" Jess asked.

"That just leaves the two boys," her father said. "Billy's the one I'm most familiar with.

They say he's pretty wild. I think both he and his brother are lifeguards, right?"

Jess nodded. She'd never actually told anyone in her family that Reed Petersen was her chair partner. From the sound of things, she wasn't about to now.

The moon was so bright, Reed imagined he could almost feel its rays on his shoulders as he sat in his jeep. He was parked on a dark street in a part of Far Hampton he'd never been to before. It was a community of small, well-kept ranch houses, not far from the highway. A place where year-round residents, not summer people, lived. According to the map and phone book, he was parked on Jess Sloat's street. Her house was the one that was brightly lit halfway down the block on his right.

What was he doing sitting there in the dark?

Reed wasn't sure. All he knew was he couldn't stop thinking about her. It had gotten so bad that he couldn't even concentrate on working on *Simplicity*. Finally he'd just gotten into the jeep and driven over here. He still wasn't certain why or what he expected to find. But here was her street and the house she lived in. It was clear that it was worlds away from the kind of life he had, but it wasn't bad in any way, it was just different.

Reed shifted slightly in his seat and listened to the chirping of what sounded like a million crickets. He could still feel her in his arms. How tired and vulnerable she'd been as she pressed her face against his chest, still gasping for breath after the rescue. How beautiful she'd looked, even with her wet hair hanging down like strings of corn silk. Even after he'd carried her halfway up the beach, he hadn't wanted to put her down. He wished he could have just kept walking . . . to some faraway place where they could be alone.

Reed glanced back at her house again. He wished he could know more about Jess's world, about what the inside of her house looked like, and where she went to school and hung out. And he wished he could show her what his life was like. Not the estate out here and the huge apartment in the city, not the prep school and European vacations, the housekeepers and cooks. But the parts he really enjoyed. Like gliding across the water on *Simplicity*, listening to jazz fusion, and taking long walks on the beach at night.

A light went on in a room that had previously been dark. Reed wondered if Jess had turned it on. He wondered if she was even home. Could he just walk up to the front door and ring the bell? Would she believe him if he said he was just driving by and decided to stop in? But how would he explain knowing where she lived?

A set of headlights appeared in his rearview mirror, but Reed didn't pay attention. A moment later the car pulled up behind his jeep. Reed turned and was momentarily blinded by a strong bright flashlight beam.

"Get out of the car slowly and put your hands over your head," a deep male voice ordered.

Reed got out of the car. As his eyes adjusted to the bright lights he recognized the markings of a Far Hampton police car. Two officers had gotten out of the car. One kept his flashlight on Reed while the other used a second flashlight to quickly inspect the interior of the jeep.

"It's clean," the cop doing the inspecting said.

"License and registration," the other cop said to Reed.

Reed slowly reached into his pocket and removed his wallet, showing them both pieces of identification. The cop inspected them with the flashlight.

"You're Charlie Petersen's son?" he asked, not hiding the surprise in his voice.

"Yes."

"Mind if I ask what you were doing just sitting here in the dark?"

"Thinking," Reed said.

The two cops glanced at each other.

"Okay, Reed," the first cop said, handing back his license and registration. "But take some advice: You're better off sitting in your car and thinking over on your side of town, okay?"

"Sure." Reed got back into the jeep and started it up. He'd have to wait to see Jess tomorrow.

Andy couldn't stop staring at the full moon. Lisa had left a while ago, but he'd stayed on the beach, just watching and wondering about things. He wondered about the moon and how on earth they'd ever managed to land someone on it. He wondered about being a senior guard tomorrow and what it would be like to command his own chair. But mostly he wondered about Jess, and whether or not to give up hope.

After what seemed like hours of wondering, he came up with no definite answer.

Finally, he knew it was late, and time to go home. The sand felt cool and damp under his feet as he walked up the dark beach with the moon at his back. Suddenly he heard a car door slam. Looking up the beach to the parking lot, he saw a pair of taillights go on as a car pulled away. He couldn't see who was driving, but in the bright moonlight he could make out the outline of the car. It was a jeep.

★   ★   ★

It was after eleven when Paula's phone rang. She was doing her toenails and watching TV. She'd just had her toenails done that afternoon in town, but those idiots never did it right so she'd taken off the polish and was doing it all over again. Now who could be calling at this hour of the night? Paula picked up the phone.

"Hello?"

"Hi, it's Billy." He sounded very serious.

"Oh, hi, what's up?"

"I did it."

Paula wasn't sure what he was talking about. "Did what?"

"Got Reed back."

Paula's heart skipped a beat. "Oh, Billy, you're serious?"

"You'd better believe it."

"You put it in his jeep?"

"No, someplace even better."

She couldn't believe he'd actually done it! "God, I don't know how I can pay you back."

"You were going to get me Jess, remember?"

Paula's elation dropped a few notches. That's right, that's what she'd promised him. "I'll see what I can do, Billy."

"You'll do better than that," Billy threatened.

"Okay, just give me some time." She slammed down the phone angrily. It wasn't going to be easy to get Jess to go out with Billy. But then she smiled. Billy had done it! He'd actually stolen that stupid radar! Oh, revenge was going to be sweet.

THIRTEEN

It was drizzling the next morning when Jess got up. As the drizzle turned to a light rain, she waited for a call from Hank telling her not to come in that day. But the call didn't come, so Jess put on a rain slicker and caught a bus to the beach.

There were two police cars outside the lifeguard shack when she got there. She quickened her pace and arrived at the door just as Reed came out. Instead of wearing his lifeguard outfit, he was wearing khaki shorts and a polo shirt.

"Hi, Jess." He looked very glum.

"Reed, what happened?" Jess asked.

"Someone stole the Doppler radar," he said.

A second later Hank came out with three policemen. He looked surprised to see Jess.

"Gosh, I'm sorry, Jess," he said. "With all the excitement, I forgot to call you and tell you not to come in."

"It's okay," Jess said.

"Now you say there was no sign of forced entry?" one of the policemen said to Hank.

Hank shook his head. "None."

"No broken windows? No pry marks around the door?" another policeman asked.

"You can see for yourself," Hank said.

"Any chance you forgot to lock up last night?" the first cop asked.

Hank shrugged. "Well, I guess there is. I mean, I've been working here for more than fifteen years and I've never done it before, but I guess anything's possible." He paused for a second. "Hey, wait. I had a couple of guards stay late. Maybe they'd remember. You can ask them."

"It just stinks," Reed suddenly blurted out angrily. "It really does. We got that radar to help protect people's lives. Whoever stole it is a total slimeball."

Jess was surprised by his outburst. She'd never seen him so angry before.

Hank turned to him. "Look, Reed, why don't you take the day off and go home, okay? Ellie and Andy are coming in. As long as this weather stays bad, they're all I need."

"You sure?" Reed asked.

"Yes," Hank said.

"But usually you keep all the senior guards," Reed argued.

"I'll be fine today," Hank assured him. Then he turned to Jess. "You, too, Jess."

The rain was turning harder. As she pulled up the hood of her rain slicker, Jess was glad she didn't have to stay. Reed stood next to the shack with his head bowed against the rain and his hands shoved in his pockets. His hair was starting to get matted down by the rain. "Hey, you need a ride somewhere?"

Jess nodded. Reed opened the passenger door to the jeep for her and then climbed in on the driver's side. He turned the key in the ignition and started the windshield wiper, but instead of putting the jeep in gear, he just sat and stared at the windshield wipers swiping back and forth.

"I wonder why Hank did that," he muttered. "He always keeps the senior guards when it rains."

"Maybe he knows how upset you are and he's just trying to give you a break," Jess said.

Reed shrugged. "I just don't get it, Jess. I don't get how anyone can put their own personal greed or needs over those of so many others."

"I wish I had an answer for you."

"It just doesn't make sense," Reed said. "I mean, it's not like a TV you can put in your house or sell to someone. That radar's good for only one thing, detecting storms. The only person who'd want it would be a weatherman or another lifeguard."

"Maybe it was just a prank," Jess said. "Someone doing it just to see if they could do it."

Reed shook his head slowly. Then he turned to her. "So where can I take you?"

The answer burst into Jess's mind before she had a chance to think. She didn't care where they went. She just wanted to be with him.

"I don't know." She turned and gazed back at him. "Where are you going?"

"Me?" Reed smiled slightly and shrugged. "I don't know. Back to the house, I guess. If it's going to rain all day, I'll try to get some work done in *Simplicity*'s cabin."

The debate that had raged in Jess's thoughts the night before tried to start up again. But with Reed so close, it was no contest. "Could I come?" Jess heard herself say, almost as if she had no control of her own voice.

Reed gazed back at her with a bemused look on his face. She wished she could tell what he was thinking. "I think you might find it pretty boring."

"If I do," Jess said, "I promise I'll tell you."

Reed drove down the beach road to the area

where the large homes were. Jess had been there before. She and her friends sometimes rode their bikes there and gaped in amazement at the huge mansions and perfectly manicured lawns behind the tall metal gates designed to keep sightseers out. Jess had never imagined that she'd ever get to go inside any of those gates. It almost seemed as if the people who lived behind them came from a different world.

But now Reed pulled up to a tall ornate black gate with spearlike tips painted gold. He pressed something that looked like a garage door opener and the gate slowly swung open. Inside the estate, Jess caught a glimpse of the broad lawns and gardens and the tall brick mansion as they drove straight to the dock where *Simplicity* was kept.

The rain fell steadily as Reed helped Jess step down into the sailboat's cockpit and then opened the cabin door for her.

"Watch your head," he said as she ducked down and stepped inside.

The cabin was dim and smelled of varnish. The air felt cool and moist. She could hear the sound of water sloshing against the hull outside. Behind her, Reed came in and closed the door. For a moment, it was dark. "Don't move until I get a light going," he said.

She waited until she saw a match burst into flames. Reed held it to a small glass lantern. As the wick of the lantern caught, she watched the warm light glow against his handsome face. Reed lit a second lantern and hung one on each side of the cabin.

Jess looked around. The cabin was small and cozy. Both she and Reed had to stay bent to keep from bumping their heads on the ceiling. There was a small table and chair against one wall, and a tiny stove and sink along the other. Beyond that, toward the bow, were two bunk beds, one on either side of the hull.

"Where do I sit?" Jess asked.

"You'll probably be most comfortable on one of the bunks," Reed said.

Jess crouched down and moved to the bed. Reed sat down on the chair beside the table. It had started raining harder outside. Rain splattered and rattled against the cabin's roof.

"So how do you like it?" Reed asked.

"It's cozy," Jess said. She crossed her arms and shivered a bit.

"Cold?" Reed asked.

Jess nodded. "What do you do for heat?"

"Wear heavy sweaters and drink lots of hot tea," Reed said, getting up from the chair. Staying in a crouch, he came toward her and bent down to open a drawer under the bunk opposite her. As he pulled open the drawer, his back was only inches from Jess's knees. Jess fought the temptation to reach out and run her fingers through his damp, chestnut-colored hair, or curl her hands over his powerful-looking shoulders and knead the muscles beneath. It was tempting, so tempting.

"Here you go." Reed pulled out a hand-knit, cable-stitched lamb's wool sweater and handed it to her. "That ought to keep you warm."

Jess squeezed the soft wool between her fingers. She'd seen sweaters like this for sale in the stores for hundreds of dollars. If she had owned a sweater like that, she probably would have kept it in her top drawer at home and worn it on every possible occasion. It was a little disconcerting that Reed kept it in his sailboat, where it probably lay for months without being worn.

"How about some tea?" Reed asked, moving back into the small galley area again.

"Okay." Jess pulled the sweater over her head and almost immediately felt warmer. She watched as Reed lit the stove with a match, then pumped some water into a small blue teakettle and put it over the flame.

"It'll just be a minute," Reed said as he opened a small cabinet above the stove and took out some sugar and tea bags.

Jess glanced at the lanterns and the gas stove. "Reed? There's no electricity?"

Reed shook his head. "I could run an electric line from the dock, but I figured, what's the point? There's no electricity in the middle of the Atlantic."

"But you're not in the middle of the Atlantic," Jess said.

"I'm not?" Reed looked up, pretending to be surprised. "Hey, you're right!"

Jess grinned. "I'm serious."

"Okay, seriously. Next summer, after I graduate, I'm going to sail to England."

"Really?"

"Yup. It's something I've wanted to do ever since I started sailing."

"You wouldn't do it alone, would you?" Jess asked.

"That depends," Reed replied. "If I can find someone who wants to do it with me, great. But if I can't, then yes, I probably will go alone."

"Have you found anyone?"

"Not yet."

Jess tried to imagine herself sailing with him.

She'd only been on a sailboat a few times, and never had to do anything except sit and watch. But she thought she'd like to learn.

"Do you just pack up the sailboat and go?" she asked. "Or do you practice?"

"You really should practice," Reed said. "It's like getting in shape. That's one of the things I haven't actually figured out how to do yet. When I'm at St. Peter's, it's really hard to get out here and sail on the weekends. Sometimes I think it would be a lot easier if I went to school somewhere out here next year. Then I could sail almost every weekend and really be ready to go when school was over."

Jess felt a sudden rush of hope and then forced it back down. If he went to school near her next year, it would change everything. Wouldn't it?

Steam was hissing out of the kettle and Reed turned off the flame and poured the steaming water into two blue ceramic mugs. He handed one to Jess. She could see how comfortable and at home he felt in the sailboat. Somehow it was easy to imagine him sitting here in the middle of the ocean, making his tea, on his way to England.

"Sugar?" Reed asked.

Jess shook her head. "No, thanks. But what

about storms?" she asked, cupping the mug with her hands to warm them.

"You always get 'em," Reed said. He dropped two teaspoons of sugar into his mug and stirred it. "If it's a bad one you can always throw out the sea anchor and batten down the hatches. This sailboat is supposed to have a water-tight cabin. According to my grandfather, the whole sailboat could turn upside down and I'd stay dry in here."

"Has it ever happened?" Jess asked.

Reed shook his head. "That's why something like the Doppler radar would be . . ." His voice quickly faded into nothing.

"What were you going to say?" Jess asked.

"I was going to say that the Doppler radar would be great because it detects thunderstorm cells early enough so that you can sail around them." Reed shook his head, suddenly glum again. "I just can't believe someone stole it. It's such a dumb thing to do."

"Can't the town get another one?" Jess asked.

Reed shrugged. "I guess, if they have insurance. Those things are pretty expensive. And it'll probably take months. They don't make a lot of them and they're in pretty high demand."

"But even if we don't have it anymore, it just means going back to the way things used to be," Jess said. "Was it that bad?"

Reed shrugged. "I guess not. I mean, besides the fact that every couple of years someone somewhere on the south shore gets hit by lightning."

"It's never happened in Far Hampton, has it?" Jess asked.

Reed shook his head. "Not that I know of." He paused for a moment and looked down at the floor of the sailboat. Jess could see it really bothered him. She wished she could reach out and put her hand on his shoulder to comfort him.

"Reed?"

"Yeah?" He looked up.

"There's something I don't understand," Jess said. "I know this may sound funny, but why do you care so much?"

He looked surprised. "Why wouldn't I?"

Jess slid as close to him as the bunk would allow. "I don't want you to take this the wrong way, but I guess what I mean is, you don't even have to be a lifeguard."

Reed stared back at her quietly. Jess was afraid she'd insulted him. Suddenly he got up and moved toward her, sitting down on the bunk opposite hers. They were so close their knees were touching.

"I don't blame you for wondering, Jess," he

said, gazing earnestly into her eyes. "I suppose a lot of people must wonder about it."

Jess nodded, feeling almost mesmerized by his nearness and intensity.

"I guess you know the story of how my father came here and bought up all this land and made a lot of money selling houses," Reed said. "My mother was always a firm believer that you didn't just take without giving something back. I guess that's where I got it from."

"So you try to give something back by being a lifeguard?" Jess asked.

"Basically, yes," Reed said. "I mean, it's what I like to do. I could probably be a lifeguard over at the Shore Club or one of those other places my friends belong to, but I'd rather do it for the people of Far Hampton. It just means a lot more that way."

Then he shrugged. "You probably think it sounds pretty hokey."

Jess was touched by his earnest attitude. Without realizing it, she put her hand down on his knee and leaned toward him.

"I think it's good," she said. "I mean, you're so different from the way I thought someone from the city would be."

He gazed back at her and she felt his hand close over hers and his face move closer.

"How did you think someone from the city would be?" he asked in a whisper.

Jess's heart was beating like a drum; she felt warm and tingly as if she were on the verge of breaking into a sweat. All the arguments against this were gone now. All that remained was a distant tiny voice cautioning her, and even that was fading fast.

"Not like you," she whispered back.

Reed's face came closer. Jess closed her eyes and parted her lips. All she could think about was feeling his lips on hers and his strong arms around her body. She felt him take her in his arms, felt his lips press firmly against hers. She felt as if she were melting into him, as if their hearts had merged and were beating as one. . . .

She thought for a moment she heard voices, then thought perhaps she'd only imagined it. She had no idea how much time had passed. She and Reed were stretched out on the bunk, his body pressing down on her, his lips caressing her face and lips, her hands in his hair and under his shirt, tracing the hard taut muscles of his back. She couldn't remember ever wanting someone so badly, needing to feel his body against hers, drinking up his kisses ravenously, never wanting to let go.

Then she heard the voices again. Only this time they were louder. Reed heard them, too, and she felt his body grow stiff and tense.

"Who is it?" Jess whispered beneath him.

"I don't know," Reed whispered back. "But whoever it is, they're not supposed to be here."

Now they could hear footsteps on the dock.

"Reed Petersen?" a voice asked. "You in there?"

"Yes, just a minute." Reed sat up on the bunk and started straightening his clothes. "Who is it?"

"The police. We want you to come out here."

FOURTEEN

"What do they want?" Jess whispered, sitting up beside him and starting to straighten her clothes.

"I don't know," Reed said.

In the flickering light of the lantern she could see the worried expression on his face.

"I guess we'd better go see," Reed said. He started to get up, but Jess grabbed his arm and pulled him back to the bunk. He gave her a questioning look, but she only pulled him closer and kissed him one more time on the lips. After a moment, Reed pulled back and smiled a little.

"Thanks."

A few seconds later, Reed opened the cabin doors and stepped outside. It was still raining and the day was gray. Three men stood on the dock. Two were in police uniforms and raincoats. The third man looked older, wore a gray suit, and was holding an umbrella. When they saw Jess follow Reed out of the sailboat, their faces filled with surprise.

"Jess?" the man in the suit said.

"Hi, Detective Ryan," Jess said, pulling the hood of the rain slicker up. She said hello to the policemen, too. She knew them both. One was Officer Brenner, the other, Officer Pfeffer. But what were they doing there?

The detective named Mr. Ryan turned to Reed. "Is your name Reed Petersen?"

"Yes," Reed said. "What's going on?"

"I'm Pete Ryan, detective with the Far Hampton police department. Can I ask you a few questions?"

"Well, sure."

The detective took a key out of his pocket. It was tied to a piece of orange cord. "Do you recognize this?"

"Sure," Reed said. "It's the spare key to the lifeguard shack."

"We just found it in the top drawer of the dresser in your bedroom," the detective said.

"What were you doing in my room?" Reed asked.

Detective Ryan took a piece of paper out of his pocket. "This is a search warrant signed by his honor Judge Herb Green about half an hour ago, giving me and my men authority to search your personal property. Would you mind if we had a look at your sailboat?"

"Uh, no, of course not," Reed said, scowling. "You didn't have to get a search warrant if you wanted to look at my sailboat. But I'd like to know what this is about."

Detective Ryan told the officers to search the sailboat and then turned back to Reed. "You were down at the lifeguard shack this morning, right?"

"That's right," Reed said.

"So you know there was no sign of forced entry in the theft of the town's new radar," the detective said.

"Well, yeah, but didn't Hank say he might have left the shack open the night before?" Reed said.

"We've spoken to two lifeguards who remember seeing him lock the door last night," the detective said.

"Oh, okay," Reed said. A vague sense of discomfort was growing over him, but he wasn't sure why. They couldn't really think he'd taken the radar, could they?

The officers came back out of the cabin. "No sign of it, sir," one of them said.

Detective Ryan nodded and then looked over

the rest of the sailboat. "What's in that hatch?" he asked, pointing at a hatch in the bow in front of the main mast.

"Just the spinnaker and a couple of extra sails," Reed said.

"Mind if they have a look?" Detective Ryan asked.

"No, go right ahead."

They all watched as one of the officers climbed over the rain-slick roof of the cabin and opened the hatch. He looked down and then reached in and pulled something up. A stunned silence fell over the group as they all realized it was the dish to the radar. Reed felt a chill run up his spine.

"Do you have any idea how that got there?" the detective asked him.

Reed shook his head. He knew Jess was staring at him with a look of shocked amazement.

"I'm sorry, Reed," Detective Ryan said, "but I'm afraid you're under arrest."

Jess watched as Detective Ryan advised Reed of his right not to speak without a lawyer being present. When the detective asked Reed to put his hands behind his back and then handcuffed him, Jess felt as if she couldn't breathe. This can't be happening, she kept telling herself. Not after what they'd just shared inside the sailboat. . . .

*   *   *

"Jess?" Chief Sloat stood in the doorway to the darkened screened-in porch.

"Hmm." Jess was staring up at the night sky. Tonight there was no moon, just dark clouds.

"What were you doing on Reed Petersen's sailboat?" her father asked, sliding into a cushioned seat opposite her.

"It's a long story, Dad."

"I've got time," her father replied.

"Dad . . ." Jess shook her head. She wasn't up to an interrogation at that moment. She was incredibly upset and confused.

"It's important," Chief Sloat said.

"Do they think I was an accomplice?" Jess asked bitterly.

"Were you?"

"Dad!"

"I had to ask, Jess," her father said calmly. "Now that you've given me an answer, I believe you."

"Gee, thanks." Jess couldn't believe him sometimes.

"Why were you there?"

"I just was, Dad. It . . . it was the first time." Jess prayed he wouldn't ask her any more questions about it.

"Did you have any idea that he'd taken the radar?"

"God, Dad, what do you think?" Jess asked angrily.

"I guess not," her father said.

Feeling tears start to well up in her eyes, Jess looked away and tried to blink them back without her father seeing. She wished he would go away and leave her alone, but he only leaned closer, propping his elbows on his knees and intertwining his fingers.

"Look, Jess," he said. "I'm sorry you're so upset. I don't know what was between you and Reed, and I'm not sure I want to. But I think there's something you should know. There are three criteria we use to decide if someone is a suspect: motive, means, and evidence. Reed Petersen qualifies strongly in all three. As for a motive, Hank Diamond himself has told us that Reed spoke about how much he'd like a Doppler radar on his boat. As to the means, he was the only person besides Hank who possessed a key to the lifeguard station. And as for the evidence . . . it's obvious, we found it on his sailboat. You might also be interested to know that two of my officers found Reed parked in his jeep in the dark last night on our street."

Jess looked up and stared at her father. "On our street? What was he doing?"

"According to my men, he said he was thinking," Chief Sloat said. "From that point until eight this morning when the housekeeper saw him, he has no alibi for where he was or what he was doing."

"What did Reed say he was doing?" Jess asked.

"He says he drove around for a while and then went home."

"Why don't you believe him?"

"Jess, if he were home, don't you think someone else in the house would have known it?" her father asked.

"Not in his house. Two people could live in there for years and not know about each other."

"You've been inside?" her father asked as his eyebrows rose in surprise.

"No, but I've seen the outside and it's huge."

Chief Sloat was quiet for a moment. Then he said, "Look, Jess, I've been in this business for a long time and I've seen a lot of cases. If Reed is innocent, he's going to have to prove that somehow another person got hold of either his or Hank's key, stole the radar, and put it in his sailboat. Not only is he going to have to explain how that could happen, but why someone else would do such a thing. Now Hank says his key is on a key ring that he never lets out of his sight. Reed's key was in the house, which as you probably know, is protected by an elaborate security system. It's not like some stranger could just stroll in there unnoticed, take the key, steal the radar, put it in the sailboat, and then put the key back."

Jess stared into the dark, wiping tears out of her eyes with the tips of her fingers. She still couldn't believe it, or could she? Had she been wrong? Had Reed been lying to her in the sailboat? Had it all been some kind of scheme to get her, the police chief's daughter, on his side in case he got caught?

"I hate to make generalizations, Jess," Chief Sloat said. "But one thing I've noticed is that a lot of these rich kids seem to have this idea that they're above the law. It's like they know their parents have enough money to hire the best lawyers and will always get them out of any trouble they get into. Frankly it's an attitude I find extremely repugnant. Reed Petersen will be prosecuted to the fullest extent of the law."

Jess had nothing to say. She felt numb. From what her father said, it seemed impossible that Reed could be innocent. And yet to think of him as guilty was a possibility too horrible to even imagine.

FIFTEEN

The next morning Hank called everyone onto the porch of the lifeguard shack before they went on duty. The lifeguard captain looked pale and shaken.

"I'm sure you've all heard about Reed," he said to the silent, stupefied group around him. "I know it comes as a shock to all of us. It's a terrible shock to me. Of all the guards I've worked with over the years, I thought Reed was the most responsible and honest of the bunch. Now I . . . well, I just don't know what to say."

The other lifeguards murmured in agreement. Jess's numbness from the night before had turned into a sickening nauseated sensation. She felt almost physically ill. She would have called in sick that morning, but she knew the crew was already one lifeguard short.

"The important thing is that we try to put this behind us today," Hank said. "When you're out

*   *   *

in your chairs, remember your first obligation is to the patrons."

As the lifeguards slowly filed off the porch, Jess saw Andy stop and wait for her on the sand. Good old Andy . . . Jess realized she'd hardly thought about him during the past week. She'd been so consumed with thoughts of Reed. But now she was very glad Andy was waiting there for her. He would comfort her and be her friend. Just like old times. She slid her arm around his waist and they walked together out onto the beach.

"Can you believe it?" he asked solemnly.

"I don't know what to believe," Jess replied.

"I can't say I liked the guy, but I still never would have believed it if it wasn't so obvious," Andy said.

"I know." Jess nodded and kept her arm tight around his waist.

As they walked together across the beach, Andy was keenly aware that this was the closest he'd been to Jess since the night she'd given him The Big Chance and he'd blown it. From that moment on, it seemed that he'd been replaced in her life by Reed. But now Reed wasn't in the picture anymore, and Andy believed that if he was smart and careful, things would go back to the way they were.

Andy thought back to the night of the full moon, two nights before. He remembered he'd seen someone drive away from the lifeguard shack in what certainly looked like a jeep. From where he stood, he couldn't tell if it was Reed driving or not, but now it didn't seem to matter. The police were convinced it was Reed. The important thing for Andy was that he had Jess back, and this time he intended to keep her.

Andy went down to the East Wing chair to sit with Lisa, and Jess stopped near the Main chair. Hank had assigned the lifeguard named Stu to be the new senior guard, and he was already up in the chair. It was a cool, hazy morning and there were no patrons on the beach yet. Jess wasn't eager to climb the ladder and join him. It was so hard to accept the fact that Reed wasn't up there.

"Jess?"

She turned around and saw Billy coming toward her.

"I just want to say I'm sorry about Reed," Billy said, acting much less arrogant than usual. "I mean, I know you and he were kind of close.

If there's anything I can do, well, don't be afraid to ask."

"Thanks, Billy." Jess turned and climbed up into the chair and sat down. What had just happened seemed very strange to her. Reed and she might have been getting close, but Billy was Reed's brother. If anything, it should have been Jess telling Billy she felt sorry. And what did he mean when he said if there was anything he could do?

Reed was out on bail. His father had hired a lawyer to represent him in the case. As soon as he finished explaining to the lawyer that he was totally innocent and had no idea how the radar wound up on *Simplicity*, Reed called Hank at the lifeguard shack and asked if he could still sit in the Main chair. After all, a person was innocent until proven guilty.

"I'm putting you on leave until this thing is cleared up," Hank replied, sounding strangely distant.

"Hank, you can't be serious," Reed said.

"I have to think about the morale of the other guards, Reed," Hank said.

"Morale? What are you talking about? Nobody thinks I really stole the radar, do they?"

"That's not for us to decide," Hank replied. "Once it's over, you're welcome to take over your old spot."

Reed hung up the phone, feeling more shaken than when the police officer had found the radar on *Simplicity*. He couldn't tell for certain, but it sounded an awful lot like Hank actually thought he was guilty.

The sun burned through the haze, and the afternoon turned beautiful. Paula tried to relax beside the pool at her parents' summer house, but she was too wired to lie peacefully and soak up the rays. So far her plan had worked perfectly, but Paula felt surprisingly uneasy. She should have been thrilled! Reed had been arrested and had no doubt been relieved of his lifeguarding duties until the case was resolved one way or the other. Poor little prim and proper Jess must have been beside herself, thinking that handsome earnest Reed was actually a thief. Paula was certain she'd have nothing more to do with him. Reed's other friends would abandon him as well. Wasn't that the perfect revenge?

Absolutely. But then why didn't Paula feel proud of herself?

Because maybe revenge wasn't what she really

wanted. Maybe what she really wanted was to have Reed back, to prove to everyone that he couldn't live without her.

She could picture him now without his beloved lifeguard job, without his friends, feeling lonely and hurt. What if Paula went to him, loving and understanding and willing to accept him no matter what? Would he see how wrong he'd been to break up with her?

Paula tried to read and listen to the radio, but she couldn't sit still. Like a criminal she was consumed with the desire to return to the scene of the crime and see firsthand the havoc she had wrought. Finally, she couldn't stop herself from getting into her car and driving to the beach.

What she found there was disappointing. As the day had turned sunny and warm, the beach had grown crowded. The lifeguards were all in their chairs. Paula spotted Jess in the Main chair, sitting with some guard she'd never noticed before. From the outside, Jess didn't appear to be grieving much. Paula sighed. Well, it was a nice day and there was no sense in going back to her pool. She picked out a good spot, and spread out her thick red beach towel, radio, and magazines. Feeling thirsty, she decided to head for the snack bar before lying down.

*   *   *

As Billy Petersen walked across the hot sand toward the snack bar, he should have felt incredibly pleased. After all, he'd had the perfect revenge. His brother had gotten him demoted from senior lifeguard, and he'd turned around and gotten Reed thrown off the crew completely. But the victory felt bittersweet. Maybe it was because he was now assigned to the West Wing chair with Ellie, who had just sent him on a gofer run for a large orange drink. Or maybe it was because he was starting to think that Paula Lewis was going to renege on her end of the bargain, namely, getting Jess Sloat to go out with him.

Suddenly up ahead in the snack line, Billy saw something that made him smile. It was the back of a skimpy red bikini. There was only one girl he knew who wore bikinis like that, and she was just the girl he wanted to speak to.

"Hi, Paula."

Paula spun around. "Oh, hi, Billy." She didn't look happy to see him.

"There's something we need to talk about," Billy said.

Paula knew exactly what that was. She'd promised him Jess Sloat, and somehow she had to deliver. "All right."

"When?"

"Uh, how about the Crab Shack after you get off work?"

"Fine."

They waited silently in line until they got their drinks. Then Paula headed back to her towel. The truth was, she really didn't have to deliver anything, and there was nothing Billy could do about it unless he wanted to go around telling everyone he stole the radar because she had told him to. But Paula would try to keep her promise, not because promises meant anything to her, but now that she had decided she wanted Reed back, she knew she was better off keeping Billy on her side.

Andy spent his first day as senior guard in the East Wing chair thinking about Jess. He knew it was pure luck that he'd been given a second chance with her. This time he wasn't going to blow it. He wasn't going to come on too strong or too fast. He'd just be there for her. And gradually she'd see that he was the one who'd always been faithful and true.

Sitting beside him, Lisa tried to read his mood. He seemed very quiet, considering how exciting this day must have been for him. She knew that they were all bummed by the news about Reed taking the radar, but still, she'd never thought of Andy as being a great friend of Reed Petersen's.

"So how does it feel?" she asked as they both sat in the chair scanning the beach and the waves.

"Huh?" Andy wasn't certain what she was referring to.

"Being a senior guard?"

"Uh, great." Andy grinned.

"Not scary?"

"No way."

"That's funny," Lisa said. "It still seems like a pretty scary prospect to me."

"Yeah, well, you're new," Andy said. He spread his arms over the back of the chair and relaxed a little. He'd been so preoccupied with thoughts about Jess all day that he'd almost forgotten that he was now a senior guard.

"So how's Jess taking the news about Reed?" Lisa asked.

"I think she's sort of upset," Andy said.

"Based on what you told me the other night, I would think she'd be more than just 'sort of' upset," Lisa said.

Andy shrugged. He really didn't want to discuss it with her now. Someone knocked on the base of their chair. Andy and Lisa looked down and saw Ellie.

"Listen, guys, I'm asking some people to get together at the Crab Shack after work to talk about Reed," she said. "I'd really like it if you two came."

Andy and Lisa said they'd be there.

Jess hadn't wanted to go to the Crab Shack, but Ellie persuaded her to. Now she, Ellie, Andy, and Lisa were sitting at a table in the bar area of the crowded restaurant, sipping sodas. Andy was eating handfuls of pretzels from a wicker basket in the middle of the table, but Jess had no appetite.

"Look," Ellie said to them. "I know you guys probably all have things to do tonight, so I won't keep you long. I just wanted to say that I've known Reed for three years. We sat together his rookie year, and I think I got to know him pretty well. He's the most honest, responsible, up-front guy I've ever met. There aren't many things I'm sure about in life, but one of them is that Reed Petersen didn't steal that radar."

"Then who did?" Lisa asked.

"I don't know," Ellie said. "But the reason I asked you guys to come here was to take a little time and try to remember everything that's happened this year." Ellie paused and looked at Jess. "Especially you, Jess."

"Why me?" Jess asked.

"Because you've been sitting with him," Ellie said. "Was there anyone he had a fight or a disagreement with? Is there anyone you can think of who might want revenge?"

Jess tried to think back over the past few weeks. There'd been many times when Reed had whistled patrons out of the water, asked them to turn down their radios, or play Frisbee in places that weren't so crowded. A couple of times he told guys not to drink beer. Then she thought of something.

"He has been having a sort of ongoing debate with Gary Pilot about where he can boogie board," she said. "But I never thought it was serious."

"Gary doesn't seem like the type who'd plot out such an elaborate scheme," Ellie said.

"I know that Reed and Paula broke up," Lisa said.

"But I heard Paula broke up with him," Andy added. "If anyone wanted revenge, wouldn't it be Reed?"

The others nodded. Once again, the memory of the jeep leaving the beach parking lot came back to Andy. He would have said something, but if anything, it just seemed to make Reed look more guilty.

Jess had nothing to add. The whole thing just made her miserable and depressed. She got up.

"Where are you going?" Andy asked.

"I just need to use the bathroom," she said and started to cross the crowded dining room. Just as she was about to go into the ladies' room, she saw something that made her stop. Paula and Billy were sitting at an outdoor table behind the restaurant, and it looked as if they were arguing.

Unaware that Jess was watching them, Paula glared across the table at Billy.

"Listen, I told you I'd set you up with Jess, and I meant it," she said in a low voice.

"When?" Billy asked.

"When I have a chance," Paula snapped. "It's only been a day since Reed was arrested. What's the rush?"

"The rush is I want to see you come through with your half of the deal before you get on some plane and go off to Greece or someplace," Billy said.

Paula clenched her teeth. Billy could make her so mad. "I'm not going anywhere! But suppose

I did? What do you think you'd do? Go to the police and tell them you stole the radar and put it on Reed's boat?"

"I'd tell them you told me to do it," Billy said.

"Oh, really?" Paula wanted to laugh. "And what do you think they'd do then? Come and arrest me? You're the one who did it, Billy. You've got no proof I told you to do it, and it doesn't matter anyway."

Billy blinked. He'd never considered it from that angle, but she was right. As far as anyone else was concerned, it looked as if he'd acted on his own. "Why you . . ."

"Relax," Paula said. "I told you I'd get Jess for you and I meant it. Just give me some time and get off my back."

Paula started to get up. Jess quickly ducked into the bathroom, not wanting to be seen. She wondered what they were arguing about. She was almost certain, from reading Paula's lips, that Paula had said something about radar and getting arrested. Why would Paula and Billy be arguing about that? Well, it could have been anything, Jess thought sadly. Or maybe Paula hadn't said radar, but something that only sounded like it.

When Jess came out of the bathroom, Paula was gone, but Billy was still sitting at the table. An idea flashed into Jess's head, but she hesitated. There was something she was dying to ask Billy, but could she really do it? Did she really want to get involved? Before the answer came to her head, she felt her feet moving toward his table.

"Hi."

Jess watched as Billy looked up at her and did a double take as if he couldn't believe what he was seeing. Then he quickly looked around. Was he looking for Paula?

"Uh, hi, Jess," he said.

Jess pointed to the seat opposite him. "May I?"

"Uh, sure."

Jess sat down. She didn't understand why she was doing this. It was probably a waste of time. Still, she gave Billy a sympathetic look. "You know this morning, when you told me you were sorry about Reed? I should have said the same thing to you."

She watched as Billy nodded uncomfortably, probably uncertain of what she was getting at.

"Billy," Jess leaned forward. "You know him better than anyone. Do you really think he took the radar?"

Billy nodded.

"Why would he do it?" Jess asked.

"I don't know," Billy said. "I guess he just wanted the radar, that's all."

"But didn't he think he'd get caught?" Jess asked.

Billy shrugged. "I guess he thought he could get away with it."

Jess nodded as if this was interesting news, but inside she was disappointed. She'd hoped that Billy would have more insight into his brother than that. Instead, Billy seemed as puzzled and uncertain as everyone else. The one thing that seemed obvious was that he didn't appear to be very sorry about what had happened to his brother. Then again, everyone knew Reed and Billy didn't get along, so maybe it wasn't that surprising, either.

"Do you think maybe he wasn't thinking clearly?" Jess asked. "I mean, maybe he was so upset because Paula broke up with him. . . ."

"Is that what he told you?" Billy looked surprised.

"Well, no, he never actually talked about it," Jess said. "But that's what I heard."

Billy smirked. He leaned across the table and spoke in a low voice. "Don't believe it. Paula thinks she's so great. She always has to make herself look like a winner. But the truth is Reed broke up with her. She's just telling everyone it was the other way around because she can't stand the thought of people thinking she got dumped."

Interesting, Jess thought, working hard to make it seem like the news meant nothing to her.

"So, uh, I guess you're still pretty upset, huh?" Billy asked.

"Oh, I don't know," Jess said. "I didn't really know Reed that well. I guess it just shows you can't always go by first impressions. So, uh, I'll see you later, okay?" She started to get up.

"Hey, wait a minute," Billy said. "You going to that fifties concert tonight?"

"I don't know," Jess said. She'd heard something about a concert over in Hanover Park near her house, but she'd been too preoccupied with Reed to think about it. The last thing she wanted to do was go with Billy, but something told her to handle this carefully. "What time does it start?"

"Around eight," Billy said. "I'm going to go over to Huntington to get a new video camera, but I'm pretty sure I'll be back in time. Maybe I'll see you there?"

"Maybe," Jess said, although she doubted it strongly.

*   *   *

Billy watched her walk away. He couldn't tell for certain, but it sure seemed like she'd been pretty friendly. And what had she meant with that thing about first impressions? It sounded like maybe she was referring to him! Well, Billy was going to make darn sure he was at the concert tonight, just in case Jess showed up.

As Jess made her way back toward her friends, she couldn't help thinking that she'd just learned something interesting. *Motive, means, and evidence* . . . That's what her father had said. If Billy was telling the truth and Reed had broken up with Paula, then Paula had a motive: revenge. And who else besides Reed had the means to get into Reed's room, take the key to the lifeguard shack, and steal the radar? His brother, Billy, of course.

But there were still unanswered questions. Why would Billy and Paula work together to set up Reed? That was a tough one. Jess shook her head. It sounded too incredible . . . a total flight of imagination.

Maybe you just don't want to accept the truth, Jess told herself. Stop making excuses for Reed. You know you're hurt and disappointed, but consider yourself lucky that it happened now and not a few months from now when things really could have gotten serious.

Jess returned to the table. Andy and Lisa were still there, but Ellie was nowhere in sight.

"Where's Ellie?" Jess asked.

"She had to go," Andy said. "Lisa and I were just waiting for you."

Jess sat down and took a sip of her soda. She still didn't know what to think. No matter how hard she tried to suppress her new theory, it just kept bubbling back into her mind. The odd thing was, she hadn't been the only one to think of it. Ellie had been talking about someone taking revenge against Reed. Finally, she couldn't hold it in any longer. "Suppose Ellie's right. Suppose someone did set Reed up?"

The memory of the jeep raced through Andy's mind again. Something bothered him about it, but he couldn't put his finger on what it was.

"You want to know what I think?" Andy said. "I think that just like every other girl on the beach, Ellie has a crush on Reed. She's been his friend for three years and it must be really hard to face the fact that the guy turned out to be a thief."

"He might be right, Jess," Lisa said. "We've

all tried to think of who could have done it. Gary Pilot's the only one we can think of, and we all know it's really not his style."

Jess nodded. "I'm sure it wasn't Gary."

"Well, then, if you think Reed was set up, who do you think did it?" Andy asked.

"I don't know," Jess said. She didn't want to tell them her hunch about Billy and Paula. First of all, it sounded crazy, like a conspiracy or something. Second, she had no proof. Third, if the rumor got out and it was true, Billy and Paula might have time to cover their tracks. Fourth, what Andy had said of Ellie was probably true of Jess. Maybe she, too, was just making up excuses to avoid believing the obvious. On the other hand . . .

"I just think it's a possibility we can't ignore," Jess said.

"Why do you even care?" Andy asked. "I mean, Reed's father's already hired lawyers to defend him."

"My father says the case against Reed looks pretty bad," Jess said. "Once it gets to court, even the best lawyers in the world might not be able to help him."

Andy shrugged. "Look, if Reed's really innocent, then I'd feel bad for him. But frankly, I think it's his problem. I don't see why you should feel like you have to get involved."

"Maybe you're right, Andy," Lisa said, "but if Jess feels this strongly, it couldn't hurt for her to at least go talk to Reed. I mean, I'd hate to see anyone get in this much trouble for something he didn't do. Maybe if they put their heads together they can come up with something."

Andy didn't look happy about it, and Jess thought she knew why. He just didn't like the idea of her and Reed having anything to do with each other. To be honest, she couldn't blame him.

Jess finished her soda. "I don't know what I'm going to do, but I guess we'd better get going."

Outside in the dirt parking lot, they got into Lisa's VW. Jess and Lisa sat in the front and Andy sat in the back.

"I know it's hard not to think of Reed," Andy said, a bit bitterly, "but is anyone going to that fifties concert tonight?"

"I must've missed this," Lisa said. "What concert?"

"There's a free fifties concert over in Hanover Park tonight," Andy said. "I heard a lot of people are going to get all dressed up in fifties clothes and go."

"Were you planning on going?" Jess asked.

"I don't know," Andy said. "It's not really my thing. I thought maybe, if you guys wanted to, we might just go take a look."

"I think it sounds like fun," Lisa said. "I'll do it."

"What about you, Jess?" Andy asked.

"I think I'll pass," Jess said.

"What're you gonna do instead?" Andy asked.

"I don't know," Jess said. "I might just hang around at home."

"Yeah, then maybe that's what I'll do, too," Andy said.

Jess looked over and saw Lisa frown. She looked disappointed and Jess thought she knew why. It was pretty obvious that Andy had mentioned the concert to see if Jess was interested, not Lisa.

A few minutes later Lisa pulled up in front of the hardware store. "You sure you don't want to go?" she asked as Andy started to get out.

"I don't know," he said. "Tell you what. If I feel like it, I'll give you a call after dinner, okay?"

"Okay."

Andy got out and closed the door. Jess noticed that instead of putting the VW in gear, Lisa just sat and watched as he walked up the stairs beside the hardware store and let himself into the apartment above.

"What's wrong?" Jess asked.

"I think he's still really stuck on you," Lisa said with a sigh.

"Why do you think that?" Jess asked.

"It's the way he doesn't want you to have anything to do with Reed," Lisa said. "I think it's jealousy."

"Either that or he just doesn't like Reed," Jess replied.

"So what are you going to do?" Lisa asked.

Until that moment, Jess hadn't been certain what she wanted to do. Then suddenly, the answer seemed clear. "Lisa," she said, "could you do me a really super favor?"

"Sure," Lisa said.

"Could you drive me over to Reed's estate?"

"Serious?" Lisa's eyes widened. "I'd love to!"

A little while later, they pulled up in front of the gate.

"How do we get in?" Lisa asked.

Jess pointed to the small square speaker on a metal tube sticking out toward the driver's side window of the car. Beneath the speaker was a white button. "Push it," she said.

Lisa reached out of her window and pushed

the button. Then she turned back to Jess. "Wow," she said. "I feel like I'm about to put in a drive-through order for fries and a shake."

"Who is it, please?" a formal voice crackled out of the speaker.

Jess leaned across Lisa's lap and spoke out the window. "It's Jess Sloat. I'm a friend of Reed's . . ." Then, as an afterthought, she added, "and Billy's."

"You'll find Reed at the dock with his sailboat," the voice replied. "Billy hasn't arrived home from work yet."

The gate opened with a creaking noise.

"You'd think they could afford to get it oiled," Lisa quipped as they drove through.

Lisa oohed and aahed as they drove down the tree-lined drive and past the mansion on the way to the dock. Jess couldn't blame her, but her thoughts were on other things. A moment later they pulled up next to the dock. Reed was sanding the deck of *Simplicity,* wearing goggles and a red bandanna like a bandit covering his nose and mouth. He was working with an electric sander that made a high-pitched whining sound. When the VW stopped, he pulled off the goggles and gazed up with that inscrutable expression of his.

"Just wait here," Jess told Lisa. "I'll only be a second."

"Okay."

Jess got out of the car and walked toward Reed, who shut off the sander and stood up, undoing the bandanna. Beads of perspiration speckled his forehead. He smiled and seemed glad to see her.

"Hey, Jess."

"How are you, Reed?" Jess asked, stopping a few feet from him. He seemed a little surprised that she didn't come closer.

"Not so great," he replied with a slightly puzzled look. "How about you?"

"I'm still sort of stunned," Jess said.

Reed wiped the sweat off his forehead with his sleeve. "What are they saying out there in gossip land?"

"Just about everyone thinks you took the radar," Jess said. Even as the words left her lips, she was surprised by the anger she felt inside. It was the anger of betrayal. That Reed had betrayed her by getting her to like him and then turning out to be such a creep. But that was only true if he took the radar, she thought. Still, until she knew for certain, she didn't want to seem too friendly.

"And what do you think?" Reed asked, staring straight at her.

"I don't know what to think," Jess replied. She watched as he glanced at Lisa in the car and then took a step closer to her.

"You serious?" he asked.

Jess nodded.

Reed stared down at the ground and shook his head. "Does everyone really think I took it?"

"Ellie doesn't believe it," Jess said.

Reed looked back up at her. "I care more about what you think, Jess."

Jess nodded. She had a question she wanted to ask him, but it was so personal. She didn't know how to ask it.

"Why would I take the radar?" Reed asked.

"I don't know."

"Then what makes you think I did it?"

Jess knew she had to ask the question. "If you didn't, then who did?"

Reed slowly shook his head. "I really couldn't tell you, Jess."

"It had to be someone who could get into your house," Jess said. "They had to go through the gate and past the alarm systems and into your room to get the key."

Reed's eyes seemed to tighten. Jess knew that by now he had to guess what she was thinking.

"No," he said sharply. "I know what you're thinking, Jess. Maybe Billy and I don't get along that well, but he'd never do something like that to me. Never. He's my brother."

Reed pulled the bandanna back up over his mouth and nose, and the goggles over his eyes. Then he turned on the sander. The high-pitched whir filled the air.

"Reed?" Jess said. "Reed?"

Either he couldn't hear her because of the sander, or he was just pretending. Jess stared back at him, feeling stung. Either way, it didn't matter. If Reed wanted to believe that Billy would never set him up, who was she to argue with him?

SIXTEEN

The sun was setting. Reed had spent the whole day working on *Simplicity*, but now it was getting dark and he had to stop. He was angry . . . angry that he'd been set up to look like a thief . . . angry that the rumor mills had started and were blaming Billy . . . angry that he'd been so short with Jess before. He hadn't meant to snap at her, but the thought of a new rumor spreading around, naming his own brother as the person who framed him, just pushed him over the edge.

Reed pulled the dusty bandanna off his face and wiped the sweat out of his eyes. What was he going to do now? Spend the night in the house alone? By hiding from the public, wasn't he just fueling the fires for more rumors? Making it look like he was guilty? Reed had no doubt the lawyers his father had hired would prove his innocence. They *had* to, because he was. He was convinced he was just the victim of a prank. Someone's idea of a sick joke.

But in the meantime, it was crazy to hide. It would be better to go out and show people he wasn't hiding, that he had no reason to hide. Besides, he couldn't help thinking about Jess. There was a free concert in Hanover Park tonight. Reed knew the park was near her house, and he couldn't help wondering if she'd be there.

It was eight P.M. As Jess did the dinner dishes by the open kitchen window, she could hear cars honking and people shouting — the sounds of a crowd gathering in anticipation of the concert just a few blocks away. All evening long the debate had raged again in Jess's head. No matter how hard she tried to force it out of her mind, it kept crawling back. What if Reed was innocent? The more she thought about it, the more certain she was that Reed would never do anything so stupid. She kept thinking back to the day they'd learned the radar was taken and how upset Reed had been. She also thought about that very afternoon and how angry he got when she suggested Billy might have set him up. That simply wasn't the way a guilty person would act.

On the other hand, what if Billy knew more

than he claimed? She knew Reed had too much faith in his brother to ever point a finger at him. She also knew that because Billy liked her, she might be the only person in the world who could find out what, if anything, he really knew.

Could she really just stay in her house and do nothing? No. Billy had said he would probably go to the concert. The next thing Jess knew, she was pulling on a tight pair of jeans and a fresh white T-shirt with rolled up sleeves. She brushed her blonde hair straight back over her shoulders. Looking over her shoulder in the mirror, she could see that it was long enough now to reach almost down to the middle of her back. She hoped Billy would like it.

The concert still hadn't started by the time Jess got to the park. The Hanover Park band shell faced a broad sloping hill that made for a natural amphitheater. In the gray light of dusk, Jess could see that the hill was covered with young families on blankets, older people on folding chairs, and teenagers milling around or sitting on the bare grass. Jess stood at the back of the crowd, hoping that Andy and Lisa had decided not to come, and searching for some sign of Billy.

She felt someone tap her on the shoulder. She

turned around and was shocked to see who was standing there. It wasn't Billy, as she'd hoped. It was Reed!

"Reed," she gasped, quickly looking around for any sign of Billy. "What are you doing here?"

"The same thing you are," Reed replied.

"But I thought you never came to things like this," Jess said.

Reed frowned. "Well, I figured that considering everything that's happened, it might be better if I made a few public appearances."

Jess couldn't blame him for feeling that way, but he couldn't have picked a worse moment. She had to get rid of him before Billy showed up. "I think that's really smart, but . . ."

"Look, Jess, about this afternoon," Reed said.

"What about it?" Jess asked.

"I just want to say I'm sorry I was so short with you. I mean, I know you're wrong about Billy, but in a way I can understand why you thought what you did. You just sort of caught me at the wrong moment."

And now you've caught me at the wrong moment, Jess couldn't help thinking. "Well, those things happen, Reed."

She still hadn't been able to think of an excuse to get away, but she had to do something. "Anyway, I hope you like the show. I've got to go talk to someone." She started away, but felt Reed's hand go around her arm.

"Wait, Jess."

She turned and looked into his dark intense eyes. He was wearing a dark green polo shirt and neatly pressed khaki slacks and his hair was freshly washed and combed. God, she just wanted to throw herself into his arms and forget about all this. But she couldn't. If she didn't go through with her plan, Reed would be found guilty of a crime he might not have committed.

"What's going on?" Reed asked.

"I don't know." Jess pretended to play dumb. "What are you talking about?"

"I'm talking about us," Reed said. "I'm talking about that day on *Simplicity*. I just apologized for this afternoon. Please don't hold it against me."

Jess couldn't have held anything against him if she'd tried. She could remember the softness of his lips on her neck and the pressure of his body on hers. She felt a wave of emotion sweep through her. If only they could run away together somewhere and just be alone with each other forever. But they couldn't. . . .

"A lot's happened since then," Jess replied.

Reed's jaw tightened. "Look, you have to believe me. I didn't take the radar."

"Then who did?" Jess asked.

"I told you, I don't know," Reed said.

Jess knew she couldn't stand there and argue with him. She had to get away from him before Billy showed up!

"Look, Reed, I really have to go," she said, pulling her arm out of his grip.

This time Reed didn't try to stop her. He just watched her disappear into the crowd. He couldn't believe it. Of all the people in the world who might doubt him, he'd never expected it from Jess.

Reed wasn't the only one who watched Jess disappear into the crowd. Paula had seen it, too. Now she made her way through the throng to the spot where Reed was standing.

"Reed?"

Reed turned and found Paula looking up at him. If possible, she'd made herself up to look even prettier than normal that night. "Hi, Paula," he said, in a flat, unemotional tone.

"Reed," Paula said, trying to look very sincere, "I've been thinking about what happened between us. I really think I've been wrong about a lot of things."

"Like going around telling everyone *you* broke up with *me?*" Reed asked wryly.

"I only did that because I was hurt," Paula said. "You have to believe me." She slid her hand around his arm and pressed herself close to him. "I know I've been really stupid and superficial lately. I don't know what's gotten into me. I guess until you broke up with me, I never realized how bad it had become."

Reed nodded silently. The crowd was starting to settle. Down on the band shell, the MC, wearing a purple shirt and sunglasses, was greeting the crowd.

"All I ask is that you listen, Reed," Paula said. "We were together for a long time. We really had fun. Remember skiing at Zermatt and sailing off Montserrat?"

Reed nodded. They'd had fun on those trips. Maybe she was right. Paula knew him well. It wasn't like Jess, who obviously had all these doubts and didn't know him at all.

"So tell me something, Paula," Reed said. "Do *you* believe I took that radar?"

"No," Paula replied. "I know you too well, Reed. I know you'd never do something like that. That's my whole point. We know each other."

He could feel her pressing against him. There

was a certain comfort in being with someone who knew you, someone you didn't have to prove yourself to. Someone who'd be there for you when times got hard.

He could feel her squeeze his arm tightly. Paula stood up on her tiptoes and pressed her lips against his ear. "Reed, let's get out of here," she whispered. "Let's go someplace where we can be alone."

She pulled his arm and Reed felt himself going with her. Why not? Paula was the only one left who believed him.

It was growing dark and Jess moved through the crowd, looking for Billy. As she stepped around the blankets filled with picnicking families and mothers holding infants, she felt horrible about what she'd just done to Reed, but she knew she had no choice. He'd never let himself believe that Billy or Paula would do something like that to him. Maybe they hadn't, but Jess knew her mind wouldn't rest easily until she knew for certain.

"Hey, there you are!"

Jess looked up to find Billy facing her. She'd been so busy trying to step around blankets and chairs that she hadn't even seen him. She quickly glanced around, praying that wherever Reed was, he wasn't watching her. Billy was wearing a black Aerosmith T-shirt and black jeans and carrying a brown paper grocery bag.

"Oh, uh, hi," she said nervously, reminding herself not to seem too eager.

"So, uh, I guess the band hasn't started yet," Billy said, seeming equally nervous.

"I guess not," Jess replied.

"Uh, you here with anyone?" Billy asked.

"Not really."

"Maybe we could sit together," Billy said.

"Well, uh, okay."

They sat down on the grass at the top of the hill and behind most of the crowd. Behind them were some trees. It was dark now, and Jess felt somewhat relieved that most people wouldn't be able to recognize her unless they were very close. The band had finally come onto the stage and started to play. Next to Jess, Billy reached into the grocery bag and pulled out a beer.

"Want one?" he asked.

Jess's immediate reaction was to decline the offer, but she realized that might make Billy suspicious. So she took a beer.

Billy reached into the bag and took out a second can and popped it open. Jess popped hers open and took a sip. *Yuck!* She hated the taste.

Meanwhile, next to her, Billy seemed to chug half his can in one gulp.

The music was loud and fun and Jess thought she even recognized a few of the tunes from the oldies station her mother sometimes listened to. Billy drank two beers. Jess had taken a number of pretend sips from her can and then discreetly poured half her beer onto the grass beside her when Billy wasn't watching.

"So how do you like it?" he finally asked while the band took a break.

"It's fun," Jess said. "You like it?"

"Yeah, sure. . . . Uh, want another beer?"

"Okay."

While Billy reached into the grocery bag to get them each a new beer, Jess poured the rest of her first can into the grass. A moment later Billy popped the tops off new ones and they tapped cans together.

"Bottoms up," he said with a grin.

Jess smiled back at him and tipped the can to her lips, but again didn't drink.

By the end of the concert, Billy had had at least six beers. As the band left the stage after the encore and the crowd started to pack up to leave, Billy stood up unsteadily and staggered off into the woods beside the hill to relieve himself and then staggered back.

"Want to go someplace?" he asked, slurring his words.

"You're going to drive?" Jess asked incredulously.

"Sure, why not?"

"Okay," she said. "Lead the way."

SEVENTEEN

Lisa had been thrilled earlier in the evening when Andy called and said he'd changed his mind about the concert and now wanted to go. She quickly washed her hair, put on jeans and a fluffy white blouse under her denim jacket, then put on a little makeup and long gold earrings.

But when she picked up Andy, he greeted her with a tight smile and asked if by any chance she'd heard from Jess. It turned out that he'd called her house and learned from Mrs. Sloat that Jess had suddenly decided to go to the concert. Lisa was crushed. It was clear that the only reason Andy had called her was to use her to get to the concert.

Once there, he spent more time searching the crowd for Jess than he did looking at the band onstage. Finally, Lisa had to say something.

"Andy, if she wanted to be with us, she would be."

Andy turned and gave her a look.

"All I'm trying to say is that maybe she wants to be with someone else," Lisa said.

"Then I want to see who," Andy replied.

That was the last straw for Lisa. She got up, pulling her denim jacket tightly around her. "I'm going, Andy."

She hoped he'd respond or apologize or something, but Andy just nodded and kept looking around at the crowd.

It's hopeless, Lisa thought sadly and walked away.

Andy was hardly aware of what he'd done to Lisa. He was like a man possessed. He knew Jess wouldn't come to the concert alone. If she was here with someone, he wanted to know who it was. But as the concert came to an end, he still hadn't found her. Was it possible that she'd lied to her mother and done something else instead?

The concert was over and Andy joined the crowds leaving the park. As he walked back along the side of the road leading from the park, a jeep passed under a streetlight nearby. Andy saw the driver's blonde hair blowing in the breeze. He did a double take and looked again. It was Jess! And Billy Petersen was in the passenger seat! But before Andy could shout or do anything, the jeep was too far ahead.

In the jeep, Jess gripped the steering wheel tightly. She'd had no choice but to insist on driving. It would have been suicide to let Billy drive in his condition. They'd gotten to his car in the parking lot. Billy had the same color jeep as Reed's, but it didn't have the St. Peter's bumper sticker on the back. Jess had told him she'd drive. To her surprise, Billy hadn't argued. Instead, he slumped into the passenger seat and popped open another beer.

"What are you doing?" Jess asked.

"What does it look like I'm doing?" Billy replied, taking a sip from the beer.

"You can't do that in the car," Jess said. "We'll be arrested."

"I'll hold it here," Billy said, holding the can between the seats where it couldn't be seen. "So, where to?"

"Home," Jess said. She had hoped to get him to talk, but he scared her too much.

"Aw, that's no fun," Billy said. "Let's go to the point."

The point was a big place for parking. At this time of night it was frequently patrolled by the police. Jess could just imagine what her father would say if he heard she'd been seen there with Billy Petersen.

"Sorry, Billy," Jess said. "Not in your condition."

Billy was quiet for a moment. Jess felt the breeze blow her hair around and smelled the salt air as she drove through town toward the beach road.

"Bet you'd go to the point if my brother was with you," Billy said sullenly.

"No, I wouldn't," Jess said.

"Just because he got caught with the radar?" Billy asked.

Jess nodded.

Beside her in the passenger seat, Billy grinned. "Well, good, he deserved it."

Jess looked over at him. "Why?"

"Because his whole life he's always had the best of everything," Billy said. "And he's always made sure I got less."

"Like how?" Jess asked.

"You name it," Billy said. "He just always has to be better than me. When we were both on the lacrosse team, he made sure he was a starter and I was second string. When we both took the same test, he always had to get a higher grade. If we're both senior lifeguards, he has to make sure I get demoted. He just always has to be better."

Jess couldn't believe what she'd just heard. "How did Reed make sure you got demoted?"

Billy laughed out loud. "Take my word for it, he did. The guy pretends he's such an up-front honest dude, but when you know him well enough you realize he's the most manipulative sneak you ever met. I can't tell you how happy I am that he finally got what he deserved. And the great thing is he'll probably never believe I was smart enough to pull it off."

Then it was him! Jess thought.

"Pull what off?" she asked as nonchalantly as she could.

"What? Uh, nothing," Billy said quickly. "Nothing at all."

Smart enough to pull it off. . . . Jess had heard the words clear as day. Pull off taking the radar and planting it on *Simplicity*. Jess was certain that was what Billy had let slip with his beer-loosened tongue. Now she just had to find some way to prove it.

A few minutes later she pulled up to the tall iron gate in front of Breezes and started to reach for the button on the speaker.

"Don't bother, it's too late," Billy said. "They turn off the speaker inside after ten."

He reached under the seat and pulled out the remote gate opener. Jess waited for him to press it and open the gate, but Billy just held it in his hand and grinned at her.

"Aren't you going to open it?" Jess asked warily.

"Maybe," Billy replied. "But first I want to know something. How come you're here? What's this all about?"

Jess answered with a shrug. "I don't know."

Billy squinted drunkenly at her. "You just all of a sudden decided you liked me?"

Jess smiled at him to cover her nervousness. "Did I say that?"

Billy started to lean toward her. "You're here, aren't you?"

Jess's first inclination was to jump out of the car and run, but she had to stay with him. Billy had come so close to admitting that he'd stolen the radar. She couldn't chicken out now.

Billy was leaning closer. Jess shrank back into the far corner of the seat. She had to stall somehow. She had to get out of there without making him mad and figure out what to do next.

Billy was crawling out of his seat toward her. His face was only inches from hers and she could smell the beer on his breath. Jess reached out and pressed her hands against his shoulders, stopping him.

Billy stared at her. "I thought you liked me."

"You're drunk, Billy," Jess said.

"So?"

"I like you better when you're not drunk," Jess said.

Billy stared at her uncertainly. Jess slowly pushed him back. "Let's get together again when you're feeling better," she said.

"You mean it?" Billy asked.

Jess smiled. "I promise." She reached for the door handle and pulled it open.

"What're you going to do?" Billy asked.

"It's a nice night for a walk," Jess said.

"Are you serious? You must live five miles from here. Let me drive you."

"Not in your condition," Jess said. "Get some sleep, Billy. I'll talk to you tomorrow."

With a combination of fast walking and slow jogging, Jess was able to get back to her neighborhood in just over an hour. All the way, she plotted her next move. She had to prove that Billy had taken the radar, not Reed. There was only one way she could possibly do it, and that was by getting Billy to confess. It sounded impossible, but she'd almost done it tonight. She had to try again. It was the only chance Reed had.

She turned into her street and checked her watch under the streetlight. Not even midnight yet. Amazing. So much had happened. Jess reached the path to her house. All the lights were off except the one in her room, which her mother always left on when she was coming home late. Jess walked quickly up the front walk and pulled open the screen door. She was just reaching into her pocket for her key when someone said, "Have fun tonight?"

Jess spun around just as a dark silhouette came out of the shadows. She was just about to scream when she realized it was Andy.

"What are you doing here?" Jess gasped.

"Waiting for you," Andy replied.

Jess pressed her hand against her rapidly beating heart. "God, you scared me."

Andy smirked. "Pretty amazing, isn't it? There was a time when we used to be best friends. Now you hear my voice and you're terrified."

"It's not that, Andy," Jess said. "It's just that it's dark and late and I wasn't expecting anyone."

Andy looked around. "You're right. It is dark

and late, and I thought you said you were going to hang around the house tonight."

"I changed my mind," Jess said.

"So what did you do?" Andy asked. Before Jess could answer, he held his hand up. "No, don't. Don't lie to me, Jess. I just want to preserve the memory of our friendship without lies. Let me tell you what you did. You went to the concert with Billy Petersen and then you drove away with him in his jeep."

"You saw us?" Jess asked in amazement.

Andy nodded. "What happened, Jess? You got a taste of the rich life with Reed and found it irresistible? You like the mansions and sailboats, huh? So now that Reed's out of the picture, you figure you'll try to hang on to it with Billy? Did he ask you to the beach party at Sandy Dunes yet?"

Jess felt herself growing angry. God, how she hated that accusing tone of voice. "Look who's talking, Andy. Ever since that night in Rafe's you've been trying to dress like a preppy."

"That's a lie," Andy said. "I just needed new clothes."

"You used to buy T-shirts and jeans," Jess said, gesturing to the clothes he was wearing. "Now all of a sudden it's khaki slacks and polo shirts."

"So?" Andy said. "I decided to change."

Behind them the front door opened and Jess's father came out wearing a navy-blue robe. "Hey, kids."

"Uh, hi, Chief Sloat." Andy swallowed.

"Hi, Dad," Jess said uncomfortably.

"Listen," her father said. "It's getting late. Try to keep it down."

"Sure, sorry."

"It's okay." Chief Sloat winked and closed the door.

Jess and Andy looked at each other in the dark. Jess could see the pain in her friend's face and it hurt her. She put her hand on his shoulder.

"Look, Andy, I don't want to fight," she said. "Not with you. Come on." She put her arm around his shoulders. They walked down to the curb and sat under a streetlight. A thousand little bugs whizzed and fluttered in the light above them, and Andy picked up a used Popsicle stick and started scraping it against the rough asphalt, making a point.

"How could you have anything to do with that creep Billy?" he asked.

Jess took a deep breath and let it out slowly. She didn't want to tell him what she knew, but it looked like she had to. "I'm almost certain

Billy took the radar. He put it on *Simplicity* so that Reed would get caught."

Andy looked at her with a dubious expression. "I knew Billy didn't like his brother, but that's a little extreme, don't you think?"

"Billy thinks Reed got him demoted from senior guard," Jess said.

Andy frowned. Then his jaw dropped. "Oh, wow! Now I get it!"

"Get what?" Jess asked.

"The day Billy got demoted, he came back to the chair and accused me of ratting on him. He said Hank knew stuff only I could have told him. I thought he was going to kill me, except I told him I didn't know anything about it. I didn't think he believed me, but then he never said another thing about it."

"But you weren't the one who told, were you?" Jess asked.

"Are you serious?" Andy said. "I'd like to live to be eighteen. Besides, you just said it was Reed who ratted."

"No, it wasn't Reed," Jess said. "Billy thinks it was Reed, but it was someone else. Anyway, it doesn't matter who told. The only thing that matters is that Billy made it look like Reed stole the radar."

"How do you know?" Andy asked.

"He practically admitted it to me tonight," Jess said.

Once again, the memory of the night of the full moon came back to Andy. Suddenly, he realized what it was that had always bothered him.

"I think you're right," he said. "I never told anyone this, but I was at the beach the night the radar was taken. I saw a jeep pulling away from the lifeguard shack, but I couldn't see who was driving it."

"Why didn't you tell anyone?" Jess asked.

Andy shrugged. "I don't know. I guess I was afraid the police would find out and make me testify about what I saw. I mean, I may not be Reed's biggest fan, but I wouldn't want to have to stand up in court and help put him in jail."

"Then it was Reed's jeep?" Jess asked.

"No," Andy said. "That's what I just realized. You know how Reed's jeep has that big St. Peter's bumper sticker? Billy's doesn't have one because he got thrown out of school. Well, the jeep I saw that night didn't have the decal."

"Then that proves it was Billy!" Jess said excitedly.

Andy shook his head. "No, it just proves it was Billy's jeep. Reed could have taken it to throw off anyone who might see him."

"But we know he didn't," Jess said.

"Yeah, *we* know, but the rest of the world doesn't."

"Then I still have to get Billy to admit that he did it," Jess said. "I'm sure if I see him again, I can get him to do it."

"You're going to see Billy again?" Andy asked, amazed. "Once wasn't enough?"

"I have to," Jess replied. "I have to prove he set Reed up."

Andy stared through the dark at her for a second. "Why?"

"Because, Andy."

"Because you're in love with him?"

Jess hadn't expected him to ask that. It was a question she'd been avoiding asking herself. Even now, she didn't want to know the answer. "It's not right to let Reed be accused of something he didn't do."

"I've told you a hundred times, Jess," Andy said. "It doesn't matter. The Petersens have the best lawyers money can buy. Even if Reed had taken the radar, they'd find a way to get him off."

"That's not the point," Jess said. "It's still not right."

"So why do you care?" Andy asked.

Jess couldn't answer him.

"Oh, man," Andy said with a sigh. He leaned his elbows on his knees and pressed his face into his hands. "It's so obvious, Jess."

"What is, Andy?"

"You're crazy about Reed," Andy said, looking up. "You'll do anything for him. Probably even risk your life."

"I just want to see justice done," Jess insisted.

Andy looked at her with sad eyes. "You really believe that?"

"Yes."

Andy stared at her for a long time without talking. Then he shook his head and slowly pressed the pointed Popsicle stick into some grass by the curb. "Okay, Jess. How do you intend to prove that Billy took the radar and not Reed?"

"There's only one way I can think of," Jess said. "I have to get him to confess."

"Right. You're going to say, 'Gee, Billy, why don't you go to the police and tell them the truth,' and Billy's going to go right down to the police station and confess."

"Of course not," Jess said. "But I almost got him to confess tonight."

"And then what?" Andy asked. "Suppose he does confess. It's just your word against his. Not exactly iron-clad proof."

He was right. Jess realized she had to come up with something better. "Okay," she said. "Suppose I get his confession on tape?"

Andy looked at her in amazement. "How?"

"I'll wear one of those little tape recorders like they do on TV," Jess said. "I've seen them for sale in Village Electronics."

"You'll *wire* yourself?" Andy stared at her as if she were crazy. "Have you gone totally psycho?"

"I have to do it," Jess insisted.

Andy pointed a finger at her. "Don't tell me you have to do it. You want to do it."

Jess reached up and took hold of his finger. "You're right, Andy. I want to do it."

Andy pulled his hand away and looked up at the stars. "Of all the people in the world to be best friends with, I had to pick you."

EIGHTEEN

When Jess got to the beach the next morning, Billy was already there, freshly showered and wearing a clean white sweatshirt over his orange Far Hampton lifeguard suit.

"Hey, Jess," he said with a big smile.

"Hi, Billy." Jess had to stifle a yawn. She was tired from sitting up late the previous night talking to Andy. "How are you feeling this morning?"

"Great," Billy said. "Nothing a few aspirin couldn't take care of. So, uh, I was wondering when you wanted to get together again."

Jess had to stall until she had time to get the tape recorder. "I have to do something with my parents tonight," she said. "How about tomorrow night?"

"Great," Billy said. "There's that big beach party at the Sandy Dunes Motel."

"Sounds good," Jess said. Guys always smuggled alcohol into the big annual summer party at the Sandy Dunes. It was like a tradition. Maybe Billy would decide to drink again. Then she'd suggest they go for a walk. That was when she'd try to get his confession on tape.

It was time to head for the chairs. Billy started walking toward the West Wing. As Jess headed for the Main chair, she saw Paula waiting there. Jess almost froze, but some reflex in her legs kept her walking forward. Paula was waiting with a big smile on her face.

"Can I help you?" Jess asked as she stepped over the rope around the stand.

"I just wanted you to know that after the concert last night, Reed took me to the Shore Club," Paula said.

The news was upsetting, but Jess tried to brace herself against anything Paula said. "So?"

"So we had an absolutely wonderful time," Paula said. "We danced and he held me in his arms. He was such a gentleman."

"I'm sorry," Jess said, reaching for the ladder. "I'd love to hear all about it, but I have to get to work. Good-bye."

She started to climb the ladder.

"Oh, there's one more thing," Paula said. "In case you were wondering, Reed already asked me to the party at Sandy Dunes tomorrow night."

Jess climbed up into the chair next to Stu. If what Paula said was true, Jess really had to wonder why she should try to get Billy's confession. It was all starting to seem so hopeless now. But knowing Paula, it might all have been a big lie.

"Hi, Jess."

Jess looked down and saw Andy at the bottom of the stand.

"Hey, Andy, how come you're not at your chair?" Jess asked.

"No patroons down there yet," Andy said. "I told Lisa I'd be a few seconds late."

"So what's up?" Jess asked.

Andy looked uncomfortable. "I think I'd better talk to you in private."

Jess turned and asked Stu if she could get off the chair for a few moments. It was one of those rare mornings when the ocean was as smooth as glass. It was still early and there weren't many people on the beach yet. Stu told her to go ahead.

Jess climbed down. Andy fidgeted a little.

"What is it?" Jess asked.

"Well, I couldn't help noticing that you were just talking to Paula," Andy said. "Before you go through with your big plan to get Billy's confession, I think I should warn you about something. Last night, after the fifties concert, my friend Donny who works at the Shore Club saw Reed and Paula there."

Jess felt a tremor of apprehension and nodded. "That's what Paula just said."

Andy bit his lip. "Well, according to Donny, they were acting like much more than close friends."

The words hit Jess like a blow. So for once, Paula had been telling the truth. "Oh, uh, thanks for telling me, Andy," she managed to say.

"I just thought as your friend I should tell you," Andy said.

Jess thanked him and climbed up into the chair. As the shock wore off, she asked herself what else she could have expected from Reed after the way she had treated him? The truth was, she understood that he might be angry with her, but she'd never thought he'd go back to Paula.

Jess stared out at the smooth ocean water glittering with sunlight. What should she do now? Give up trying to prove it was Billy who took the radar? Leave it up to Reed's lawyers to get him off? After all, why should she get involved now? Why should she care?

Because she did. Maybe Andy had been right last night. Maybe she even loved Reed. And even if Reed never came back to her, she still wanted to do this for him.

The rest of the day passed without event, except for Gary Pilot, who wanted to boogie board in the restricted area again. This time Jess was friendly but firm with him, and Gary actually took no for an answer. Jess couldn't help wishing Reed had been there to witness it. She knew he would have been proud of her.

As soon as work was over, Jess got Lisa to give her a ride into town. She was determined to go through with her plan, even if Reed decided to stay with Paula forever.

Next to her, Lisa was unusually glum and quiet as she drove.

"Something wrong?" Jess asked.

"No."

"Then why have we been sitting at this stop sign for the past three minutes?" Jess asked with a smile.

Lisa suddenly looked up and realized she was right. "Oh, God, I'm sorry."

"You don't have to apologize," Jess said. "But you could tell me what's bothering you."

"It's Andy," Lisa said. "Last night he called up and asked if I wanted to go to the concert with him. I was so happy, I got all dressed up. And then when we got there, he spent the whole time looking for you."

"Oh, no, I'm sorry," Jess said.

"Why should you be sorry?" Lisa asked. "It's not your fault. It's mine. Of all the guys I could have liked, I had to pick him. I always do this. Sometimes I just want to give up."

"Don't," Jess said. "I really think if you give it time, he may come around."

"You're serious?" Lisa looked at her with wide eyes.

Jess nodded. Sooner or later Andy would have to realize that nothing was ever going to happen between him and her.

"I'm just wondering how much time I have to give it," Lisa said with a sigh. "I mean, it's almost August. The summer's half over."

"Well, I can't tell you what to do," Jess said. "I can only say that of all the guys I know, Andy is most worth the wait."

Lisa could only roll her eyes. "I hope you're right, Jess."

They reached town. Jess asked Lisa to drop her off outside Village Electronics. Inside she bought a small tape recorder about the size of a pack of cigarettes, and a tiny microphone on a long, thin wire.

She was just about to leave the store when Reed walked in. For a moment, they stood frozen, staring at each other in the doorway. All the feelings and emotions Jess had been working so hard to suppress began to swirl and boil inside her. She had to fight the growing urge to throw herself into his arms. Finally, a few words slowly found their way out.

"Hello, Reed."

"Hi, Jess." Reed seemed very subdued.

"How are you?" Jess asked. She knew he still had to be mad at her for giving him the brushoff last night. But how could she explain that she'd been waiting for Billy?

"Okay. How are things with the crew?" Reed asked.

"Pretty good."

Reed nodded. It seemed to Jess like they had no more to say, but there was something she had to ask.

"Paula told me you took her to the Shore Club last night," she said.

Reed looked surprised. "She did?"

"It's true, isn't it?" Jess knew it was because of what Andy had told her, but she just wanted to see what Reed would say.

Reed simply nodded. For a moment he wondered why Paula would go out of her way to tell Jess that. It was obvious, wasn't it? Paula was just making sure Jess knew she and Reed were back together again. Reed couldn't help smiling to himself. Paula had sworn to him she was going to change, but she hadn't. Not one bit.

"Are you two back together?" Jess asked.

"Why do you want to know?" Reed asked. "Last night it looked like you didn't care who I was with."

It's not true! Jess wanted to shout. But she couldn't say a thing. She just stared back at him. "Reed, I . . ." she began, but didn't know how to finish the sentence. Reed looked puzzled.

"Paula said you're going to the Sandy Dunes with her tomorrow night," Jess said.

"So?" Reed replied.

"I . . . I might see you there. Late." Jess couldn't stay there another second without bursting into tears. She hurried around him and ran out of the store.

Fighting the intense desire to run after her, Reed watched her leave. He wished he understood her. He wished he understood what was going on.

NINETEEN

The following afternoon after work, Jess got Andy to go back to her house and help her get ready.

"I can't believe I'm doing this," Andy grumbled as Jess stood with her back to him and pulled up her blouse.

"This is what friends are for," Jess said, teasing him. All day she'd alternated between moments of total depression, elated anticipation, and total fright at what she planned to do tonight.

"Yeah, right," Andy said sourly. "Now hold still and keep the recorder against your back."

Jess felt Andy press the cold little tape recorder into the small of her back. She reached behind herself and held it there while he secured it in place using a thick roll of adhesive tape.

"You sure it won't come loose?" Jess asked.

"Not if I do this," Andy said. Jess felt him reach around her, pulling a strip of tape around her stomach. "That ought to hold it," he said. "Just don't let him get his hands inside your shirt."

"Andy!" Jess gasped. "What kind of girl do you think I am?"

"The crazy kind to be doing this," Andy said. He plugged in the microphone cord and passed it around her. "Where are you going to hide it?"

"Right in the front of my bra," Jess said.

"Need help positioning it?" Andy asked.

"No!" Jess slid the little microphone up under the bra between the cups. Then she quickly tucked the blouse back into her jeans before Andy got any other ideas. Andy showed her how to reach behind her back and press the record button.

"It'll tape for half an hour," Andy said. "And frankly, if you have to spend more than that alone with Billy, you're in big trouble."

"I know," Jess said, feeling a tremor of nervousness. She quickly looked at herself in the mirror. She'd put on blush and heavy eye shadow tonight . . . more than she normally used. But she was going to use everything she had to get that confession out of Billy. She turned back to Andy.

"Ready?"

Andy had a funny look on his face. "You totally sure you want to do this, Jess?"

Jess nodded.

"Even though you know Reed's going to the Sandy Dunes with Paula tonight?"

"Yes," Jess said.

"If Billy catches you, he could get pretty rough," Andy said.

"He's not going to catch me," Jess said.

Andy gave her another look. This one was very sincere. "Okay, here's all I ask. No matter what happens tonight, you have to come back to the party so I know you're okay. I'm not going to leave until you're back and I know you're okay."

Jess tried to smile. "Thanks, Andy."

Andy shook his head in wonder. "I hope you know what you're doing."

So do I, Jess thought.

A second later they heard the beep of a high-pitched car horn outside. It was Lisa, there to give them a lift to the party. Andy and Jess went out and got into the VW. Jess found the adhesive tape tugged uncomfortably at her skin, and when she sat, the corners of the little tape recorder pressed painfully into the small of her back.

"How come you wanted to go so early?" Lisa asked as they drove toward the beach. "We'll probably be the first ones there."

Jess glanced back over the seat to Andy. Before she left the beach that afternoon, Jess had told Billy to meet her at the party early. She was hoping they could leave before Reed and Paula arrived, especially since Paula always had to get everywhere fashionably late.

"Jess just can't stand missing a single second of the fun," Andy said.

"Well, I hear there's going to be a really good band," Lisa said. "And people dance right on the beach."

"It's a regular blast," Andy said. "The only thing they don't supply is the fire water." He reached into his back pocket and pulled out a silver flask. "We have to supply that ourselves."

In the rearview mirror, Lisa watched as Andy unscrewed the top of the flask and took a pull.

"Want some?" Andy held the flask out to them. Jess could smell the strong scent of alcohol.

Lisa and Jess looked at each other and shook their heads.

"No, thanks," Lisa said. "But just out of curiosity, what is it?"

"Rum," Andy said. "Good for rum and Cokes."

"Wow," Lisa said. "I guess it's really going to be a wild time tonight."

You're not kidding, Jess thought.

TWENTY

Lisa was right. They were practically the first ones at the party. The band was still setting up on a platform on the beach, and motel employees were rolling out large plastic garbage pails filled with ice and sodas. The smell of charcoal lighter fluid was in the air as cooks lit the grills upon which they'd cook hundreds of hot dogs and hamburgers that night.

"I sure am glad we got here so early," Lisa said, deadpan.

Jess was already looking around for Billy, but it was Lisa who saw him first.

"Oh, God, look who's coming," she groaned. "Too bad there's no crowd to get lost in."

Jess and Andy gave each other a look.

"It's okay, Lisa," Jess said. She smiled at Billy as he came across the sand toward them.

"Hey, everybody," Billy said. "Ready for a big night?"

"Not yet, but I will be," Andy said, taking a Coke out of one of the garbage cans. As the others watched, he popped open the top, poured some soda into the sand, and then refilled the can with rum from his flask.

"Hey, that's the spirit," Billy said, taking out a flask of his own and imitating Andy. He held the can filled with rum and Coke out to Jess. "Want some?"

"Sure." Jess took the can and took a small sip.

"Jess!" Lisa gasped.

"What?" Jess said, handing the can back to Billy.

"I didn't know you drank."

Jess smiled. "It's a party, isn't it?"

Lisa looked completely confused, which was understandable. Jess made a subtle motion to Andy, who quickly got the message.

"Hey, Lisa," he said. "Have you ever watched someone cook three hundred hot dogs?"

"Sounds really thrilling," Lisa replied, rolling her eyes.

"If you've never seen it," Andy said, slipping his arm around her waist, "you don't know what you're missing."

Jess watched Andy lead a mystified Lisa away. She owed him one for that. She turned back to Billy. "You look nice tonight."

"You look pretty good yourself,' Billy replied, staring hungrily at her.

Jess felt a moment of dread. Somehow, it was a lot easier to imagine getting Billy's confession than it actually was to do it.

Billy drank three rum and Cokes. It was dark by now and the band had started to play. Billy was staring at the band, nodding his head to the music and in no rush to leave, but Jess knew it was crucial to get away before Reed arrived.

"Come on, Billy," she said. "Let's go."

"What's the rush?" Billy asked. "This band is good."

Jess knew it was time to do the unthinkable. She slid her arm around Billy's and pressed her lips toward his ear. "I was thinking of going to the point."

Billy turned and stared at her with wide eyes. "Oh, yeah? Well, in that case!"

The next thing Jess knew, she and Billy were walking arm and arm toward the motel parking lot. It was still early and a lot of people were arriving and walking in the other direction toward the beach. Jess just prayed she didn't run into anyone she knew.

"Jess? Billy?"

Jess felt a shiver run up her spine. It was Reed's

voice. There he was, standing ten feet away with Paula. And there she was, arm in arm with Billy.

"Hey, bro," Billy said with a malicious grin.

On Reed's face was a rare look of total shock. Jess watched as he caught himself and tried to hide it.

"Well, don't you two make a swell couple," Paula said with a nasty smile.

"What is this?" Reed asked.

"What does it look like?" Billy asked back with a victorious smile.

"Jess?" Reed couldn't hide the hurt, perplexed look on his face. *Then he did care!* Jess's heart leapt, and then practically broke for him when she realized there was nothing she could do or say now.

Meanwhile, Paula tugged on Reed's arm. "Come on, Reed, can't you see they're leaving? They're probably going to the point."

Jess watched in silent horror as Paula led Reed away. Reed kept looking back at her and Billy as if he just couldn't believe what he was seeing. Now she knew she had to get Billy's confession at any cost. If she didn't, Reed would never understand.

Once again, Jess told Billy she was going to drive. The one consolation about going out to the point this early was that no one else would be there. They'd all still be at the party.

Billy was quiet on the way out. The paved road that led to the end of the point ended at an overlook on a cliff over the ocean, but no one who wanted to park ever drove that far. All the way out there were little unpaved turnoffs. On a Saturday night after midnight, almost every turnoff had a car parked in it. Jess turned off into the first one she came to. She wanted to get this over with as fast as possible.

The turnoff went through some brush and trees and ended near the edge of a low rise, with a pretty view of the dark ocean speckled with moonlight. Jess stopped the jeep and put on the brake. She was too preoccupied to even think about the vista.

"I can't believe we ran into Reed," she said.

"Yeah, pretty funny look on his face," Billy gloated.

Jess felt her hands squeeze the steering wheel hard. Then she got control of herself. "I guess you're pretty pleased with yourself," she said, turning toward him and reaching around to her back to flick on the tape recorder.

"It's about time that guy got what he deserved," Billy said.

"I thought he already got what he deserved," Jess said. "When they found the radar in his boat."

Billy grinned. "Then this is just icing on the

cake." He turned toward her. "So here we are, just you and me, alone in the dark at the point."

Jess nodded nervously. Once again, Billy started to lean toward her. Only this time she knew she couldn't push him away. Not if she wanted to get what she needed.

"Do you think it's enough?" Jess asked.

Billy looked uncertainly at her. "Is what enough?"

"That it's enough for Reed," Jess said. "I mean, so what if they caught him with the radar? My friends say your father has lawyers that can probably get the charges dropped."

"Hey, you think I care?" Billy asked and leaned closer toward her. "Not as long as I get what I want."

"I just feel like what you said the other night was right," Jess said. "He really does get whatever he wants. If the charges for stealing the radar get dropped and he's back with Paula, it's like nothing's really happened to him."

Billy hesitated, then smiled. "Okay, you want to know the truth? It's not that easy. He's gonna have a hard time getting off on those burglary charges."

"Even with your father's lawyers?" Jess asked.

"Yeah, we set it up too tight," Billy said with a satisfied grin.

"What do you mean, we?" Jess asked wonderingly. "You don't mean you were behind it, do you?"

Billy just smiled. "You don't think my brother, Reed the angel, would really steal that thing, do you?"

"So you set it up to make it look like he did?" Jess asked, pretending to sound delighted.

Billy's grin was a mile wide, but all he did was nod. The tape recorder couldn't record a nod. Jess had to get him to admit it.

"I don't believe it," she gasped. "How did you do it?"

"Doesn't matter," Billy said, leaning closer toward her. "The only thing that matters is it's done and he's in deep." He reached over and pulled her toward him. Their faces were only a few inches apart now. "Now, how about it, Jess?"

Jess wasn't sure that what he'd said was enough of a confession to convince anyone. Meanwhile, Billy came closer. Just as he was about to kiss her, she squeezed her hand up onto his shoulders and held him back.

"Just tell me how you did it, Billy," Jess said. "I'm dying to know."

Instead of answering, Billy suddenly pulled her against him and pressed his face against hers.

"Stop, Billy!" Jess tried to squirm away as

Billy tried to kiss her, but he held her down with one hand while he slid his other hand up her blouse. *"Billy!"*

"Playing hard to get, huh? I thought you Far Hampton girls were supposed to be easy." His breath was hot and smelled of rum. He pressed her against the seat roughly. Jess could feel his hand sliding upward toward her bra. She couldn't get him to stop.

"No! Stop!" she cried.

"Give up, Jess," Billy growled lustily. "You didn't drive me all the way out here to back out now."

Jess desperately searched for an excuse to stall.

"Please, Billy, not yet. You're too fast. It's too soon."

"Not too soon for me," Billy replied with a laugh. "I've been looking forward to this since the summer began."

The next thing Jess knew, his hands were all over her. She was trying to fight him off, but he was too strong and he had her pinned. She felt his hands go over her bra and pull as if he were trying to rip it right off her.

Suddenly his hand stopped almost directly over her heart. She could feel it thumping against his hand. But there was a small hard object between his palm and her skin.

"What the . . . ?" Jess felt Billy's hand close over the microphone and pull hard. A second later he brought it up to his eyes. "A microphone?"

Jess tried to twist away, but Billy's other hand closed hard around her neck. Each time she tried to move, he squeezed hard, choking her. Now with his free hand, Billy started to feel around her body. He discovered the tape across her stomach and followed it around to the small of her back.

"Ow!" Jess cried out in pain as Billy pried the small tape recorder away from her skin and inspected it.

"I should have known," he said, shaking his head. "It was too good to be true."

Jess stayed frozen, certain that any second now he would turn his wrath on her. Still holding her with one hand, Billy slipped the tape recorder into his pocket. Then he turned to Jess.

"Reed get you to do this?"

Jess shook her head. "He doesn't know anything about it."

Billy squeezed her throat harder. "You sure?"

"Yes, I swear," Jess gasped. "You saw the look on his face before."

"Yeah, you're right." Billy loosened his grip on her throat. "Too bad your father's the chief of police and Reed saw us leave the party together. Otherwise I could bang you up pretty good and it would just be your word against mine."

"What are you going to do?" Jess asked.

Billy grinned. "I'm not gonna do anything. And neither are you. I don't know how you found out I took the radar, but you have no proof. It's just your word against mine. And all the evidence supports me." Once again Billy tightened his grip on her throat. "And I wouldn't go starting rumors, either. Because you never know what could happen. Maybe sometime this winter, or next spring, one day when I'm supposed to be away at school, you'll be walking alone somewhere and something really bad will happen to you. And no one will ever know who did it."

The next thing Jess knew, Billy reached past her and pushed open the jeep's door. And then he pushed her out.

TWENTY-ONE

Jess walked through the dark back down the road that led from the point. It seemed as if she'd been doing a lot of walking around at night lately. Her hip throbbed where she'd hit the ground after Billy pushed her out of the jeep, but other than that she was okay. Physically, at least. Emotionally she was a wreck. There was nothing she could do now to prove to Reed that Billy had set him up. And after that scene in the parking lot, Reed would probably never want to speak to her again anyway.

There was a car coming toward her. Jess imagined some couple inside heading for a secluded spot. Her heart ached worse than her hip. There was a time when it might have been she and Reed driving to the point. But now she'd lost Reed forever.

The approaching car slowed and stopped. Jess saw the red and blue plastic rack of lights on top and realized it was a police car. The driver rolled down his window? "Jess?"

It was Officer Pfeffer. "What are you doing out here?"

"It's a long story," Jess said.

"Can I give you a ride home?" Officer Pfeffer asked.

"How about over to the party at Sandy Dunes Motel?" Jess asked.

"Okay, Jess, if that's what you want."

A few minutes later Officer Pfeffer dropped her at the motel. The parking lot was still filled with cars and Jess could hear the loud music of the band. She felt a sense of dread. The party was the last place she wanted to go. She didn't want to see Reed and Paula, or anyone else for that matter. She just wanted to go to her room and hug a pillow and cry.

But she'd promised Andy she'd come back and let him know she was okay. He said he wouldn't leave until she did. And after all he'd done for her, she couldn't let him down.

As Jess stepped onto the beach she saw a group of boys in wetsuits carrying boogie boards. One of them was Gary Pilot. Despite her misery, Jess felt a small, sad smile crawl onto her lips.

"Gary?" she said.

Gary stopped, with a surprised look on his face. "Oh, uh, hi, Jess."

"What are you guys doing?" Jess asked.

"Uh, nothing." A sheepish smile appeared on Gary's face.

"Going night boogie boarding?" Jess asked.

"Yeah!" said one of Gary's friends. "To live music. It's like the ultimate!"

"Shut up, dummy!" Gary hissed at him. "She's a lifeguard."

"So what?" said another boy. "She can't stop us. This isn't even her beach."

"Gary, do you know how dangerous this is?" Jess asked. "There's no one on duty. You have no idea what the currents are like. And with this loud music, no one would ever hear a call for help."

Gary sighed and hung his head a little. Then he turned to his friends. "She's right, guys. Come on, let's go."

His friends looked shocked.

"Are you serious?"

"Gary, you can't listen to her."

"Aw, what a bummer!"

But Gary prevailed and led the small band of boogie boarders back toward the parking lot.

Jess smiled, but the satisfied feeling lasted only

a second. Then it was time to turn around and head back into the crowd, searching for Andy.

She found him standing with Lisa at the edge of the crowd watching as couples danced barefoot in the sand.

"Jess!" he gasped when he saw her. "What happened?"

Jess just looked back at him sadly and shook her head.

"Uh-oh, something went wrong," Andy guessed.

Jess nodded. She couldn't fight the tears any longer. She could feel two cold-hot streams creep down her cheeks.

"Oh, here." Lisa held out the sleeve of her denim jacket. "Everyone wipes their tears on this sleeve."

"Thanks." Jess sniffed and wiped her eyes.

"What happened?" Andy asked.

Jess glanced cautiously at Lisa.

"It's okay," Andy said. "I told her all about it."

"He caught me," Jess said with a sniff.

"Did he confess?" Lisa gasped.

Jess nodded. "I had it on tape, but he found the recorder."

Andy stared at her. "He *found* it?"

Jess nodded.

"How?" Andy asked.

"You don't want to know," Jess said.

"Well, I can guess," Andy said, angrily. "Next time I see that guy I'm going to kill him."

The band had started playing a slow number. In the crowd of dancers Jess picked out Reed and Paula dancing close, Paula's head pressed against his chest, her eyes closed. Jess felt every last bit of hope drain out of her. Her heart felt leaden.

"So Billy knows you know," Lisa said.

"Yes," Jess said. "I'll never be able to get him to confess now."

In the crowd of dancers, Paula opened her eyes and her gaze met Jess's. Paula stretched up toward Reed and whispered something in his ear. Reed turned and looked at Jess for a long moment. Then he looked away.

Jess stared down at the sand. She felt as if her heart were crumbling into a thousand little pieces.

Andy could see how shaken she was. He turned to Lisa and whispered that it might be best if he and Jess could be alone for a few moments. Lisa understood. She said she felt like going for a walk along the beach anyway.

Andy put his arm around Jess's waist and led

her away from the dancers. As they walked along the sand, a light evening breeze cooled the tracks of the tears that had run down her cheeks.

"You really like him, don't you?" Andy said.

"Yes." Jess sniffed and her body trembled.

"I've never seen you like this over a guy before," Andy said.

"I've never been like this over a guy before," Jess admitted.

Andy stopped her and turned her to face him. "Jess, I have to ask you about something. Remember that night a couple of weeks ago? When you kind of said it might work between you and me? What happened to that?"

Jess reached up and put her hand on Andy's shoulder. She looked sadly into his eyes. "Good old Andy," she said softly. "You're such a good friend."

"What about that night, Jess?"

She shook her head. "I'm sorry, Andy. It was just wishful thinking."

"That's all?" Andy had a pained expression on his face.

Jess nodded. "You're my best friend, Andy. You'll always be my best friend. That night I thought it could be great if it could be more, but I was just fooling myself."

Andy stared down at the sand for a long time. Then finally, he looked back up at her. "So what do you think you'll do now?" he asked.

Jess shrugged and glanced back at the party. She felt a small, sad, crooked smile form on her lips. "Be a lifeguard, what else?"

Andy walked back toward the crowd. Jess had said she was going up to the motel to call for a cab to take her home. He stopped by one of the large plastic garbage cans and fished around in the ice-cold water until he found a Coke. He popped it open, poured half of it away, and then emptied his flask into it. He took several big gulps and felt a shiver as the mixture burned a path toward his stomach.

Reed Petersen is the biggest fool who ever lived, he thought angrily.

The slow dance had just ended. Andy felt his feet propelling him through the dancers as he searched for one couple in particular. There they were, Reed and Paula, strolling off by themselves. Andy lurched toward them.

"Excuse me!" he said, slurring his words.

Both Reed and Paula turned and stared at him with surprised looks on their faces. Without warning, Andy reached back and swung hard at Reed's chin.

He missed and stumbled past Reed, falling to his hands and knees on the sand. Jeez, can't I ever do anything right? he wondered as he staggered to his feet and raised his fists again.

"You're drunk, Andy," Reed said calmly.

"No, kidding, Einstein!" Andy staggered forward and tried to charge him like a wrestler. Reed managed to sidestep him and once again Andy tumbled to the sand. Only this time Reed followed from behind and pinned Andy's arm behind his back, pressing the side of his face into the sand.

"Hit him, Reed!" Paula shouted. "Beat him up!"

"You'd like that, wouldn't you, Reed?" Andy grumbled as he spit sand out of his mouth. "One way or other you just want to beat the crap out of all the townies."

Andy tried to struggle out of Reed's grip, but Reed held him down tight. A small crowd of kids gathered around them.

"What are you talking about?" Reed asked.

"Don't pretend you don't know!" Andy shouted. "You guys just think you can take everything you want from us. Our town, our land, our girls. . . . You don't even know how lucky you are. You don't even know what you've got. You don't deserve her."

He could feel Reed stiffen.

"You know who I'm talking about, don't you?" Andy shouted. He watched as Reed glanced at Paula. "I'm talking about Jess, you idiot!"

Reed felt his hands ball into fists. If this kid didn't stop calling him an idiot . . .

"She loves you, pea brain!" Andy shouted at him.

"That little manipulative witch!" Paula hissed behind them. "She talked you into this, didn't she, Andy?"

"Shut up, Paula," Reed said. Then he turned back to Andy. The crowd was watching them. Reed grabbed Andy by the collar and pulled him down the beach.

"If she loves me," he said in a low voice, "how come she acts like she can't stand me? How come she went with Billy tonight?"

"Because she found out Billy took the radar," Andy said, pulling away from him.

"That's a lie!" Paula shouted.

Reed turned and saw that she'd followed them. He glared at her. "How would you know?"

"I, uh . . ." Paula stammered.

"She went with Billy because she wanted to

get him to confess," Andy said. "But to do it she had to make him believe she hated you. It was the only way she could get Billy to trust her."

"Did Billy confess?" Paula gasped.

"Jess says he did, but he found out what she was doing and got the tape," Andy said.

"Then there's no proof," Paula said, turning to Reed. "Don't believe him, Reed. He's making the whole thing up. He's Jess's friend and she's making him do this to try to get you back."

"Listen," Andy said to Reed. "The last thing in the world I want to see is you two together, understand? The only reason I'm telling you this is because it's the truth. If it were up to me, Jess would never talk to you again. But the only thing that ticks me off more than the idea of you two together is seeing Jess so miserable."

"I can't believe Billy would do it," Reed said.

"Well, I've got news for you," Andy said. "I was at the beach the night the radar was taken. I saw a jeep pull away from the lifeguard shack. I never told anyone because it sounded like you were already in enough trouble. But then I remembered something. The jeep I saw didn't have a St. Peter's bumper sticker on it."

Reed didn't want to believe it. His own

brother set him up? It was almost the worst sin imaginable. But deep in Reed's heart, he'd had his doubts from the beginning. Who else could have gotten the key, taken the radar, and put it on *Simplicity*?

"Andy," he said. "You swear you saw that jeep? You swear this is true?"

Andy nodded. "Believe me, I wish it wasn't."

"He's lying," Paula gasped.

Reed stared at her for a moment, and then turned and walked away.

Jess waited near the motel office for the cab. A row of yellow lights in front of the motel rooms beside her attracted swarms of bugs and moths. The band had finished playing and was replaced by taped music for those who wanted to stay late. Jess could hear the loud, excited voices of kids as they left the beach in groups, and the sounds of engines revving and tires squealing as they headed out for the night's next adventure.

But she was going home . . . alone. There'd be no more adventures for her that summer.

"Jess?"

She looked down past the row of motel rooms. Reed was standing at the end.

"What?" she said.

"Andy told me about Billy and what you were trying to do," Reed said, walking toward her.

Jess shook her head sadly. "I can't prove anything."

Reed came close, then put his arms around her and pulled her to him. "You don't have to, Jess."

TWENTY-TWO

They lay on the soft cool sand and kissed. A lot of people were still around, but Jess didn't care who saw or what they said. She only cared that she was back in Reed's arms, feeling his soft lips against hers and his warm breath against her neck.

"You should have told me," he whispered, pressing his body hard against hers.

"I tried, but you wouldn't listen," she whispered back.

"You're right," Reed said. "It was too hard for me to believe."

Jess squeezed him and whispered, "Oh, Reed, I really thought it was over. I never thought you'd talk to me again."

Reed hugged her. "Neither did I."

They kissed again, then Jess swept his hair out of his eyes and traced his handsome face with her fingers. "What are you going to do?"

"I'll take care of it tomorrow," he said, kissing her again and again. "Once Andy tells the police what he knows, it'll change things."

"Will that be enough?"

"Yes." Reed pressed his finger against her lips. "Don't worry."

"But I *am* worried, Reed."

Reed slid his fingers through her hair and brought his face close to hers. "It doesn't matter now," he whispered. "Nothing else matters now. We're together, Jess. That's the only thing that counts."

Jess kissed his mouth and his face. "I'm just so scared something will separate us again."

Reed pulled her close and wrapped his strong arms around her. "That won't happen, Jess. I promise you."

Reed held her as tight as he could. Down the beach, illuminated by the moonlight, Jess could see a group of boys boogie boarding in the waves. She should have known better than to think that Gary would give up without a fight. Well, there was nothing she was going to do about it now. The only thing that mattered at the moment was that she was in Reed's arms and she never wanted to leave again.

★　　★　　★

She lost track of the time and was only vaguely aware that the music had stopped and the sounds of the crowd had gradually diminished. Reed held her close, their arms and legs entwined. They were quiet for a long time.

"Are you okay?" Jess whispered, pressing her face against his neck.

"Huh? Oh, yeah." Reed squeezed her.

"What are you thinking?" Jess asked.

"I . . ." Reed shook his head.

"Tell me, Reed. Please?"

"I've never felt this way, Jess," he whispered.

"Never?"

"Not ever."

They shared a long, slow, lingering kiss. To Jess, everything was perfect, like a dream. . . .

And then suddenly there were distant panicked voices coming from down the beach:

"What are we gonna do?"

"Find someone. Call the police!"

"From where?"

"The motel. Run! The rest of us will go back in."

Reed and Jess sat up.

"What is it?" Jess asked.

Reed stood up and pointed down the beach. In the moonlight, Jess could see the boys who'd been boogie boarding. Two of them were running toward the motel. The rest were in the water searching frantically.

"Something's wrong," Reed said and started running down the beach. Jess followed a few feet behind.

"What's going on?" Reed shouted as he neared the group.

"It's Gary," a kid shouted back. "We can't find him."

"You sure he's out there?" Reed shouted.

"Yeah, we all saw him get hammered by a wave. Then he never came back up."

Reed started to pull off his shirt. "We've got to find him!"

Jess stood at the edge of the dark water and watched as Reed dove into the surf. Suddenly, it was as if her brief dream had ended, and a nightmare had begun.

Don't miss *Lifeguards*

SUMMER'S END

Driven apart by a tragic accident at the beach, Jess and Reed think they let their feelings get in the way of their jobs. Now they're both up for grabs. Or at least that's the way it appears. . . .

Now Jess is hanging out with Andy, trying to keep her cool while Andy tries to keep her away from Reed. Paula is determined to win Reed back. She'll do whatever it takes — and it looks like it's working. She won't stop until she gets her way.

Billy is out for revenge, and this time he's being smart about it. He's using Paula to convince Jess that her closest friends are betraying her. Soon he'll have Jess all to himself. . . .

About the Author

Todd Strasser is an award-winning author of many novels for teenagers. Among his best known are *Friends Till the End*, *The Accident*, and *The Diving Bell*. He also wrote Scholastic's novelizations of *Home Alone*™ and *Home Alone II*™.

In addition to writing, Mr. Strasser is also a frequent speaker at schools and conferences. He lives with his wife and children just a block from the beach.

THE SUN IS HOT ...
AND SO ARE THE GUYS ON
FAR HAMPTON BEACH.

Especially Reed. Jess can't get him out of her mind.

Then his snobby girlfriend, Paula, shows up. Paula always gets what she wants.

But not this time... if Jess can help it.

DON'T MISS

Lifeguards

LG1192

NIGHTMARE HALL

where college is a scream!

High on a hill overlooking
Salem University, hidden
in shadows and
shrouded in mystery sits
Nightingale Hall.

Nightmare Hall, the
students call it.

Because that's where the
terror began.